Suz

I want to thank the very talented Jessica Fischer for the cover art.

I so appreciate Bruce Curran, who is always ready and willing to answer my cyber questions; Jayme Maness for helping out with the book clubs; and Peggy Hyndman for helping sleuth out those pesky typos.

And, of course, thanks to the readers and bloggers in my life, who make doing what I do possible.

Thank you to Randy Ladenheim-Gil for the editing.

And finally, I want to thank my husband Ken for allowing me time to write by taking care of everything else.

Aileen

Books by Kathi Daley

Come for the murder, stay for the romance.

Zoe Donovan Cozy Mystery:

Halloween Hijinks
The Trouble With Turkeys
Christmas Crazy
Cupid's Curse
Big Bunny Bump-off
Beach Blanket Barbie
Maui Madness
Derby Divas
Haunted Hamlet
Turkeys, Tuxes, and Tabbies
Christmas Cozy
Alaskan Alliance
Matrimony Meltdown
Soul Surrender
Heavenly Honeymoon
Hopscotch Homicide
Ghostly Graveyard
Santa Sleuth
Shamrock Shenanigans
Kitten Kaboodle
Costume Catastrophe
Candy Cane Caper
Holiday Hangover
Easter Escapade
Camp Carter
Trick or Treason

Reindeer Roundup
Hippity Hoppity Homicide
Firework Fiasco
Henderson House – *August 2018*

Zimmerman Academy The New Normal
Ashton Falls Cozy Cookbook

Tj Jensen Paradise Lake Mysteries:
Pumpkins in Paradise
Snowmen in Paradise
Bikinis in Paradise
Christmas in Paradise
Puppies in Paradise
Halloween in Paradise
Treasure in Paradise
Fireworks in Paradise
Beaches in Paradise – *July 2018*

Whales and Tails Cozy Mystery:
Romeow and Juliet
The Mad Catter
Grimm's Furry Tail
Much Ado About Felines
Legend of Tabby Hollow
Cat of Christmas Past
A Tale of Two Tabbies
The Great Catsby
Count Catula
The Cat of Christmas Present
A Winter's Tail
The Taming of the Tabby
Frankencat

The Cat of Christmas Future
Farewell to Felines
A Whisker in Time – *September 2018*

Writers' Retreat Seashore Mystery:
First Case
Second Look
Third Strike
Fourth Victim
Fifth Night
Sixth Cabin
Seventh Chapter – *August 2018*

Rescue Alaska Paranormal Mystery:
Finding Justice
Finding Answers
Finding Courage – *September 2018*

A Tess and Tilly Mystery:
The Christmas Letter
The Valentine Mystery
The Mother's Day Mishap
The Halloween House – *July 2018*

Haunting by the Sea:
Homecoming by the Sea
Secrets by the Sea

Sand and Sea Hawaiian Mystery:
Murder at Dolphin Bay

Murder at Sunrise Beach
Murder at the Witching Hour
Murder at Christmas
Murder at Turtle Cove
Murder at Water's Edge
Murder at Midnight

Seacliff High Mystery:

The Secret
The Curse
The Relic
The Conspiracy
The Grudge
The Shadow
The Haunting

Road to Christmas Romance:

Road to Christmas Past

Chapter 1

Monday, June 11

Some secrets are meant to be shared, others are better off forgotten.

Sixteen-year-old Naomi Collins disappeared on April 12, 2002. She'd been a troubled teen living in a dysfunctional home, and most people assumed she'd simply run away to start a new life in a new town under an assumed name. In theory, I suppose that made sense. Based on the information I'd been able to dig up, Naomi had been brought up in a home fraught with alcoholism, abuse, and long periods of abandonment. She was the only child of a hard, sadistic man, a fisherman by trade, who, according to witnesses, beat and berated his weak and timid wife whenever the mood struck.

Shortly before Naomi disappeared, her mother suffered a nervous breakdown and was voluntarily admitted to a psychiatric facility. Naomi was left alone with her father, who, it was said, spent more time in the local pub than at home. Naomi was an average student who seemed to enjoy school, although she had few friends. I assumed that was a byproduct of her father's refusal to allow her to engage in social activities other than an occasional event sponsored by the high school.

So, why, you might ask, if this missing persons case seemed to be cut and dried, would I spend an entire week of my six-week vacation in the seaside town of Cutter's Cove investigating some random girl who'd lived in town before I'd ever set foot on the sandy shore of the majestic Oregon coast? The answer to this understandable question began, as so many events in my life have, with a dream.

"You're up early," Mom said when she joined me on the deck of the mansion she and I had renovated when we first lived in Cutter's Cove. The historic home was not only magnificent structurally but perched on a bluff overlooking the Pacific Ocean. It was the perfect place to while away a lazy day.

"Couldn't sleep," I answered with a yawn as I watched seagulls glide over the aqua ocean, searching for their morning meal.

"I'm sorry to hear that," Mom sympathized as she sat down on a lounge chair next to me. We both sipped our coffee from sturdy ceramic mugs as we waited, along with my dogs Tucker and Sunny, for the sun to peek its brilliant head over the horizon. It was nice to be here in this place together again after so many years. Mom and I had first moved to Cutter's

Cove twelve years ago, after I witnessed a gangland shooting that landed my mother and me in the witness protection program. I thought the transition would be difficult, and it was, at first. But then I met my new best friends, Trevor Johnson and Mackenzie Reynolds, and suddenly, a middle-class life didn't seem so bad. For two years, I lived here as Alyson. Then, seemingly out of the blue, the murderers I had run from were eliminated by their own family, and my new life in Cutter's Cove was no longer a necessity. After a long discussion, Mom and I decided to go back to New York, where I went to college and, after graduation, went on to work for a top advertising firm as a graphic artist. Mom bought an estate in the country and, for the most part, we were happy. Still, there was a part of me that would always belong to Cutter's Cove. I just didn't know how literal that actually turned out to be.

"Are you feeling all right?" Mom asked.

I reached my arms over my head, yawned again, and let out a long sigh. "I'm fine. It's just the dream I've been having for the past few nights that's been keeping me awake."

"Dream?" Mom asked as she turned toward me and angled her head slightly to the side.

"It's a long story," I said, and I realized my fatigue was evident in my voice. I leaned back, closed my eyes, and ran my fingers through Shadow's long black fur as the waves crashing in the distance soothed me.

"I'd like to help. Especially if you feel this is more than a simple dream. Do you think it's a portent?"

I opened my eyes and momentarily considered my mother. She was one of the few people who knew about my power to see ghosts and, occasionally, glimpses of the future in dream form. She was one of the few people in my life who knew everything about me, the normal and the strange, and never judged. If there was anyone I could always talk to, it was her. "No," I answered, "not a portent exactly. I think I'm being drawn into something that took place in the past." I adjusted my position on the chaise so I was sitting up straight rather than leaning back, as I had been. "The dream always starts off with me walking up a long, narrow trail that leads from a parking field of some sort, then climbs up to a bluff overlooking the sea. It's foggy and visibility is limited. Basically, during the walk, all I can see is what's directly in front of my feet as I go. It occurs to me as I make the journey that something's very wrong, and that I should turn back. Yet, despite my own thoughts about doing just that, I continue to walk. It's almost as if I'm being pulled along against my will."

"It sounds frightening."

"Not so much frightening as heavy. I feel as if I'm carrying a great weight, and the farther down the path I go, the more burdened I become. As I continue, I'm aware of a tightness in my chest. My breath comes in gasps and there's a feeling of fear blanketed by a sort of acceptance. When I get to the top of the bluff, the fog clears. I pause to look around. I find not only a gorgeous view but an abandoned gravesite marked by a handmade wooden cross. The fear I've been experiencing on the hike up is replaced with a deep sorrow that cuts my soul."

"And the grave? Do you have a sense of who's buried there?"

I shook my head. "I don't know for certain, but recently, I've been picking up the name Naomi. I did some research and discovered a Naomi Collins disappeared from Cutter's Cove sixteen years ago."

"You think the grave in your dreams belongs to Naomi Collins?" Mom asked.

I lifted one shoulder. "Maybe. I don't have a sense that Naomi is dead necessarily, but I do know she grew up in a very unhappy home. I spoke to Woody," I said, referring to my friend, Officer Woody Baker. "Officially, it's assumed Naomi ran away. And maybe she did. Based on what I've been able to find out, she certainly had reason to. But the more I look into things, the stronger my intuition is that it's Naomi's grave I'm dreaming about."

"Talk to Woody again," Mom suggested. "He can look in the area you sense and find out who, if anyone, is buried there."

"I'd do that, but I don't know where the grave is. I see it in my dream, but though I've tried, I can't figure out the exact location of the bluff in my dream. Woody's already shared with me everything he knows about Naomi, which isn't much."

"Maybe if you have the dream often enough, eventually you'll develop a sense of where the bluff is," Mom offered.

I stretched my long legs out in front of me. "That's what I'm hoping, although I hope it happens soon. I'm exhausted. I'm ready for the dreams to stop messing with my sleep." If I was honest, I'd gotten very little sleep since I came back to Cutter's Cove three weeks ago to track down the killer of an old friend.

Mom stood up. "I'll make us some breakfast and you can fill me in on what you know to this point. It's Monday. Do you think Trevor will be by?" Mom was particularly fond of one of my two best friends. "He mentioned coming for breakfast on his day off."

"I'll text him to confirm, but if I know Trev—and I do!—he won't pass up the opportunity for some of your cooking."

Mom smiled. "I enjoy cooking for that boy. He's always so appreciative."

Not really a boy anymore, I thought to myself but didn't say aloud. "We all enjoy your cooking. In fact, I think it's one of the reasons Mac's arranging to come back to town so quickly. She doesn't want to miss out on any of the delicious meals she knows you'll be cooking while we're here."

"Do you know when she plans to arrive?" Mom asked about Mackenzie Reynolds, who currently lived in California.

"Last I heard, she's flying in on Wednesday, but I'll check to make sure her plans haven't changed."

After Mom went inside, I returned my attention to the sea. The sky grew bright as the sun began to poke its head over the horizon. We'd had rain overnight, and the lingering clouds were brilliant with shades of red, orange, pink, and purple. God, how I'd missed this place. Yes, I'd been busy with my life in New York and hadn't dwelled on what I'd left behind, but the longer I was here, where I'd been the happiest, I wondered if I could bear to leave. Mom owned the house, and I had more than enough money that I didn't need to work. From that standpoint, staying in

Cutter's Cove wouldn't be a problem. But if I decided to stay, there were other things to consider. I had a job I enjoyed and a boyfriend I was fond of but probably wouldn't miss. Mom had her own life in New York, and I doubted she'd want to stay here all the time, but she'd visit as often as she chose.

As each day passed, I wondered more and more whether my life was here in Cutter's Cove, with my dogs and my cat, and Trevor. California was a short flight away, so Mac would be able to visit often. I didn't know whether Alyson Prescott, the part of me who'd stayed behind in this house when I left Cutter's Cove and had appeared when I'd returned for a short visit, would somehow magically make her way back inside me if I recommitted my life here. When I'd first arrived and found my teenage self running around the house as if she were a real person, I was less than thrilled, but now that I'd gotten used to her, I thought if we eventually reconnected, I'd miss her. I hadn't mentioned the idea of staying to anyone yet. I wanted to come to a firm decision before I did.

"We should take a photo of the sky and the sea," Alyson said, and there she was, as if thinking about her had made her appear, and hopped up on the railing that separated the deck from the sharp drop to the sea below. "It's exceptional this morning. I bet Mom will want to paint it."

"It is an exceptional sunrise." I smiled at the apparition who was in a lot of ways just like me, yet in many others very different. "Where did you come from? I haven't seen you in days."

Alyson frowned. "Really? It doesn't feel as if I've been away. I think maybe we're beginning to merge for short periods of time."

"Merge?"

"You said you hadn't seen me, but I've known what you saw, felt, even thought, so I must have been with you."

"You can do that? Pop in and out?"

"I guess. I'm not certain, but I know things I only could if I'd been with you. Yesterday we had lunch with Trevor. He had a burger and we had a seafood salad. A woman Trev knows came over to our table and sat in his lap. He was polite but pushed her off, and the whole time we were thinking how satisfying it would be to pull her fake platinum hair out by the roots."

Now it was my turn to frown. "You're right. I think maybe I need to talk to Chan again." Chan, the magic shop owner, seemed to know what was going on between Alyson and me a lot better than I did. "I thought at some point we'd just get slapped back together. I imagined it as a single move, not a gradual assimilation."

"You know we can't merge for good unless you decide to stay here," Alyson pointed out.

I tucked my bottom lip into my mouth and nibbled on a corner. "Chan did say that."

"And I know you've been considering it," Alyson added.

"I have," I admitted.

"Not surprising. We love it here. Even though you only lived here for two years, in your heart, Cutter's Cove is home."

I acknowledged the truth in that. "It *is* home and I do love it, but I have a job and a boyfriend to consider."

"A job you've tired of and a boyfriend you know you won't miss if you never see him again. A boyfriend you were thinking of breaking up with anyway."

Alyson really could read my mind. It was a little disconcerting, even if she *was* part of me. "Can we change the subject?"

"Sure." Alyson waved her hand in a panoramic gesture. "Don't forget to take the photo for Mom."

"Hang on a sec." I got up and jogged into the house, where I'd left my Nikon. I could have taken the photo with my phone, but this sunrise deserved special treatment. I took dozens of photos, changing lenses, filters, and perspectives several times. Mom would have a lot of good options to choose from. It was too bad she'd gone in to get dressed before the big show had begun.

I think one of the reasons I'd gone into graphic design was because of my love of working with shapes, colors, angles, and light. Mom was an artist both as a hobby and a part-time profession, so I supposed I'd inherited my artistic instincts from her. She was a genius with a paintbrush, but I'd found the medium I enjoyed most was photography. Catching the perfect image at just the right time and in the right light truly was an art form not everyone understood.

In addition to taking photographs, I enjoyed creating images, layering colors and shapes until I had an image almost as lifelike as an actual photograph. I used those images to enhance the ads I created, which had made my skill as a graphic artist a widely sought-after commodity. I supposed if I did move to Cutter's Cove permanently, I could convert Mom's art studio in the attic into a photography studio in which I could create and sell my photographs and graphic images on the internet.

"Do you think the sky looks like this from the other side?" Alyson asked as she leaned her head against her chin while enjoying the colorful show taking place over the sea.

"You mean if we were in a plane looking down on the clouds from above?"

"I guess."

"I've been in a plane during cloudy sunsets. I can't say I've ever experienced a sunrise blanketed by clouds. The sunsets I've seen from the air were colorful, although nothing like this. I guess we'd have to ask a pilot who flies a lot. It's an interesting question."

Alyson floated over to the chair Mom had vacated and sat down. "I keep thinking about the girl in your dream. I feel as if we should be able to connect with her if she's dead."

"Maybe if we find the grave, we'll be able to connect."

"So, we *are* going to look for it?" Alyson asked.

Coming to a decision, I nodded. "We're absolutely going to look for it."

By the time I went upstairs, showered, and dressed, Trevor had arrived. The pizza parlor was closed on Mondays, so I assumed he planned to spend the day with us, as he had every Monday since I'd been here. He'd seemed happy to go along with whatever I'd wanted to do, so I hoped he'd be willing to help me research and attempt to locate the grave I'd been dreaming of.

"Was an effort made to find Naomi when she first disappeared?" Mom asked as she set the food on the table and we dug in.

I took a sip of my juice before answering. "I asked Woody to pull the original police file. It was one of Naomi's teachers, not her father, who reported her missing. The teacher, Elena Goldwin, told Darwin Young, the officer who was in charge then and has since retired, that Naomi had missed a whole week of school, which was highly unusual for her. When Ms. Goldwin called the father to see why she was out, he said Naomi was visiting an aunt who'd recently had a baby and needed her help. Ms. Goldwin made a comment about Naomi doing her schoolwork from the aunt's house, so she wouldn't get behind, and the father more or less told her to mind her own business and hung up. That was when she called the police and spoke to Officer Young."

"Sounds fishy," Trevor commented as he helped himself to a second serving of pancakes and bacon.

"I agree," Mom said, topping off their coffees. "Did Officer Young follow up?"

"According to Woody, Officer Young went to speak to Naomi's father. It was at that point that he admitted they had argued when he'd come home drunk the weekend before and she'd taken off. He was sure she'd be back when she cooled off a bit, so he hadn't reported her missing. He also admitted Naomi didn't have an aunt, pregnant or otherwise."

"So her jerk of a father killed Naomi and dumped the body," Trevor said.

"Officer Young thought so," I responded, "but he couldn't prove it. Naomi's body was never found and a thorough search of the house, the property, and the outbuildings surrounding the house, didn't turn up blood or any other physical evidence. Naomi's father insisted he hadn't laid a hand on his daughter, and Officer Young had no way to prove he had."

"Were other suspects considered?" Mom asked.

I nodded. "A few. In my opinion, and in Woody's, the case was dropped much too quickly because Young was so sure the father was guilty. I'm not saying that if Naomi is dead her father didn't do it; I'm just saying there wasn't a lot of effort put into finding alternatives."

Trevor refilled his glass of milk and took a sip. "Okay, so Officer Young didn't look at a lot of other suspects, but he did look at a few. Who?"

"Three other people were interviewed. The first was a boy she went out with earlier in the week. Her father didn't allow her to date, but he'd gone on an overnight fishing charter up north, and Naomi used his absence as an opportunity to go out and have some fun. The boy's name was Greg Dalton. He was a high school jock who could have dated pretty much anyone he wanted. Given the huge gap in social ranking between Dalton and Naomi, it was widely assumed by the other students Officer Young spoke to that he'd only asked her out as some sort of a joke or dare. Officer Young was never able to confirm it, but he did learn from one of Dalton's ex-girlfriends that anyone who went out with the star receiver on the football team had better be prepared to put out. The consensus was that if Naomi refused to sleep with him, he wouldn't have taken it well."

Trevor frowned. "So Dalton might have killed her for not sleeping with him?"

"He might not have been willing to take no for an answer and forced himself on her, killing her accidentally during the course of a rape. Officer Young was never able to prove it, and Dalton never admitted to any wrongdoing, so the idea never went anywhere."

Mom forked up a strawberry. "That poor girl. It sounds like she lived a dark, painful life. If she's alive, if she did simply run away, I hope she found happiness."

I hoped that as well, but somehow, I didn't think this story was going to have a happy ending.

"Who else did Officer Young look at?" Trevor asked.

"Two other men in the community. One was Frank Joplin, a homeless man who hung out by the wharf. The weekend before Naomi first missed school, she was seen talking to him near Hammerhead Beach. Connie Arnold, a classmate of Naomi and a very good friend of Greg, was the person who reported witnessing the conversation. Officer Young suspected the girl was just trying to give him another suspect to help Greg out, but he tracked down Joplin and spoke to him anyway."

"And…?" Mom asked.

"He told Officer Young he didn't remember speaking to the girl, but he noted that Joplin was wasted most of the time and didn't seem to remember much of anything. It was Officer Young's conclusion that Joplin was probably not responsible for any wrongdoing in connection with Naomi's disappearance, but he was never able to confirm he wasn't involved either because he couldn't provide an alibi."

"And the other man?" Mom asked. She was literally sitting on the edge of her chair.

I took a sip of water and continued. "The next local man to be interviewed was Jeffrey Kline, a music teacher for the middle school who also gave private lessons. It seems Kline and Naomi struck up a friendship while she was in the school. She desperately wanted to study music, but her dad wouldn't allow it, so, based on what Kline told Young, he would sometimes give her a piano lesson either before or after school. After she moved on to high school, Naomi would go to his home from time to time when she could sneak away. Kline assured Officer Young that nothing inappropriate went on, but a few of Naomi's peers stated there was a rumor that he was trading his services as a teacher for sexual favors. Officer Young wasn't able to prove it one way or another, and Kline left Cutter's Cove shortly after Naomi disappeared."

"Do we know where he is now?" Trevor asked.

"He lives on the peninsula about four hours north of here." Once I'd finished disseminating the information I'd gathered, we fell into an introspective silence. Whether Naomi was murdered or simply ran away, it was hard to deal with the fact that this poor girl had suffered so much during the sixteen years she'd lived in town. Woody hadn't been a cop when all this went down, so all he really had were the notes Darwin Young left behind. Based on what we knew, it didn't sound like the girl had a single happy day in her seemingly short life.

"What happened to the father?" Trevor asked. "Does he still live here?"

I nodded. "He does, in the same house he lived in with Naomi. He still fishes for a living and spends most of his free time in one of the local bars."

"Seems if he were guilty he would have left the area," Mom suggested.

I tilted my head just a bit. "Perhaps. We don't know for certain that Naomi is dead, and even if she is, we don't know that her father was responsible. It would seem, however, that if he were guilty of a brutal crime, he would want to move on, but a lot of killers stay put in the same place where the murders they carried out were committed."

The room fell into a momentary silence as we tried to deal with a possible killer still living in the community.

"What about the mother?" Mom asked. "You said she was in a mental health facility when Naomi went missing. Is she still alive?"

"Yes. After a couple of years of therapy and a steady drug regimen, she seemed to be much better. Collins divorced her after Naomi disappeared, and she's since remarried. She lives about an hour south of Cutter's Cove. She, along with a few people who went to school with Naomi and still live in town, are on my list of people to interview. I planned to start with what I have today."

"I'm totally in," Trevor said.

Tucker let out a single sharp bark and Sunny ran around the room, chasing Shadow. It seemed I had the beginning of my old sleuthing team to help me with what I was sure was going to be a complex mystery to unravel. Now all we needed was Mac and her tech know-how and we'd hopefully have everything we needed to accomplish what Officer Young had been unable to do years ago.

Chapter 2

When Bodine Collins had divorced his wife, Amelia, she had kept the Collins name, though she changed it when she married Timothy Landry. Amelia Landry lived with her second husband and his two children from a previous marriage in a small seaside community about forty-five miles south of Cutter's Cove. When I called and asked if I could speak to her, she'd been hesitant. I supposed I didn't blame her for wanting to bury that part of her life in the past. But I'd utilized my best persuasive skills, and eventually, she'd agreed to meet with me and me alone.

After Mom had seen the photos I'd taken of that morning's sunrise, she was itching to get the colors on canvas, so after a bit of discussion, she decided she was staying home to paint and would keep an eye on the dogs. There were three people Trevor knew at least casually who were on my list of Naomi's classmates and were still in town, so he offered to talk to them while I made the trip south. Alyson wanted to go with me, but I thought it might be best if she stayed at the house with Mom. Trevor and I planned to meet back at the house when we were finished with our tasks.

The drive from Cutter's Cove to the unincorporated town where Amelia Landry lived was one of the most beautiful in the area. The coastline south of Cutter's Cove was mainly uninhabited so the road, which hugged the sandy shoreline, was undisturbed with the exception of a few random buildings along the way. The day had begun with clouds from the overnight rain, but once the sun had risen high in the air, the last of the haze had burned off and the sky was brilliant, with sunshine that bore down and glistened on the aqua water fringed with white lapping gently on the coarse sand.

One of my very favorite trinket shops was along this stretch of coast. Years ago, I'd spent many an hour looking over handmade pottery, driftwood furniture, and locally painted seascapes. I was tempted to stop now to see if it was still there, but I didn't want to be late for my meeting with Naomi's mother, so I drove on past, promising myself to stop on my way back to Cutter's Cove if I had the time. It occurred to me, as I slowed to navigate a winding stretch of road, that I might be able to frame my better photos and sell them on consignment in the shops that littered the coast from California to Washington.

As I pulled onto the narrow street Mrs. Landry had directed me to, I found a quaint lane lined with large trees that provided shade in the summer. Each tree seemed to belong to a well-maintained if small house, which was either painted white with sky-blue trim or sky-blue with white trim. I found the uniformity somewhat tiresome, but all the homes had custom landscaping that provided enough diversity that the area as a whole was actually quite charming. I slowed as I searched for the house with the number 632 over the garage. Once I found it, I parked my Mercedes on the street, locked the door, and started up the winding path through a bed of yellow and red roses toward the front door. I rang the bell and waited.

"Ms. Parker?" the thin woman who answered the door asked.

"Yes, I'm Amanda Parker. And you're Mrs. Landry?"

The woman nodded before opening the screen door and allowing me in. "I only have a few minutes," she warned.

"I know. You said as much when we spoke earlier. I'll be quick, I promise."

She led me down a wide hallway to a living area at the back of the house. She indicated I should have a seat on the navy-blue sofa. I sat down, but not before noticing the photographs displayed on a long shelf that had been tacked up over the large window that looked out toward the yard in the back. "Is this your family?" I asked.

Amelia nodded. "That's my Timothy with his son Thomas and his daughter Samantha."

"Do you have any photos of Naomi?" I wondered.

"No. The photos we had are still in the possession of Naomi's father. Now, how can I help you?"

"As I told you on the phone, I'm looking into Naomi's disappearance. I understand you were dealing with issues of your own and not living in the family home when Naomi went missing, but I hoped you might have some insights that might help me to find the answers I'm seeking."

Mrs. Landry narrowed her gaze and studied me for a minute, then asked why I was interested after all this time. "You aren't a reporter or one of those TV folks who look at cold cases?"

"No," I assured her. I'd given some thought to how to answer this question, which I was sure would come up, and had decided to tell the truth. Or at least a partial truth. "I've been having a recurring dream. I don't know for certain yet, but my instinct is that it's about Naomi. I know that sounds odd, and I understand if you think my interest is unwarranted, but I feel compelled to try to find out what happened to your daughter."

"You think she's dead."

I paused before I answered. "I'm not sure. I think it's a possibility based on what I know."

Mrs. Landry looked down at her hands. I could see this conversation was hard on her, and I was sorry about that. The last thing I wanted to do was to cause her more grief, but perhaps if I could answer my questions, I might be able to help her find the closure she most likely wouldn't any other way. After a moment, she began to speak. "The officer who investigated Naomi's disappearance believed Bodine killed her. He came to speak to me at the facility where I was staying and basically said as much. I tried to explain to him that while he was a cruel man who drank too much, slept around, and ruled the house with an iron fist, he couldn't and wouldn't kill Naomi."

I folded my hands in my lap. "How can you be so sure?"

She looked up at me. "Bodine loved Naomi. He didn't love me, but he did love her. Sure, he was strict with her, and he didn't know how to show affection or compassion, but he loved his daughter. We both did. She was the bond that kept us together all those years."

"I understand Naomi and her father argued the weekend before she went missing."

Mrs. Landry nodded. "Naomi was a passive child. She didn't like conflict and mostly just went along. She'd learned how to deal with her father. She knew what set him off and went out of her way to avoid those things, and she did what she was told so he never had reason to find fault with her. But, like me, I think when her father came home drunk that last time, she lost it a little. I think she took off to make a life for herself elsewhere."

"What do you mean, like you?" I wondered.

"Three weeks before Naomi disappeared, I went a little crazy. That used to happen to me from time to time, but that was worse than any of the others. I'd come home from working a double shift and found Bodine in our bed with a woman who belittled and berated me every time our paths crossed. I knew he cheated, and most of the time I just let it go, but for some reason, on that particular day, it hit me as being very wrong. I started yelling and throwing things. The woman tried to leave, but I attacked her. Bodine managed to knock me to the floor, but not before I'd scratched deep welts into her face. A neighbor called the police, and I was arrested. My court-appointed lawyer thought I would benefit from therapy, and he set it up. I guess some of the tests came back wrong. I was told they indicated a much deeper problem than they'd anticipated. I agreed to go to the mental health facility for observation and testing, and Bodine's woman agreed not to press charges."

"So you think Naomi might have had the same mental illness that the tests showed you had?" I asked, surprise evident in my voice.

"The officer said she yelled at Bodine and then stormed out. He said she ran off and didn't come back. That wasn't like Naomi. That wasn't like her at all. She was a good girl. She'd never have yelled at her father unless the craziness took her over the way it took me."

I was so stunned, I had no idea what to say. Based on what I'd learned from Woody, it had appeared to me that Bodine Collins had emotionally and physically abused his wife for most of their marriage, and on the one occasion she'd lashed back at him, she was convinced it was a sign she was crazy? And if Naomi lashed out at her father, she was crazy as well? I took a moment to regroup, then said, "You don't believe your ex-husband killed Naomi. Where do you think she went?"

"I don't know for sure. It just seems likely she ran off. The only thing I'm sure of is that her father didn't kill her. I don't have any more time. I'll see you to the door."

After I thanked Mrs. Landry, I returned to my car and headed north. Talk about an interview going exactly the opposite of the way I expected. I knew Naomi's mother had remarried, so I guess I assumed she was now mentally stable, but from what she'd just said, I was beginning to doubt that. I wondered if she'd left one domineering man for another. She'd been married to Timothy Landry for eight years, and yet I hadn't seen a single photo with her in it in any room I'd been in. All the photos in the living area were of Landry and his children. I wouldn't be a bit surprised if she hadn't gone looking for another man to dominate and subjugate her after her marriage to Collins ended.

I'd wanted to try to shake some sense into the woman, but it wasn't my place. Besides, I didn't have the whole story. In fact, I reminded myself, all I really had on which to base my suppositions was a short, tense interview about the daughter she'd lost at what had to have been one of the lowest points in her life. I really needed to work on my tendency to be judgmental about the choices made by others. Especially in instances like this, where I had only a single sliver of information on which to base an opinion.

I turned the radio to a station playing classic rock. The drive back toward Cutter's Cove was as lovely as the one down had been, and I was determined to enjoy it. The sun shining on the salty sea made it appear as if little diamonds floated on the surface. Spending the day investigating a girl I believed was buried in the grave I'd been dreaming about seemed an important thing to do, but part of me wished I could chuck the whole idea and go surfing instead.

By the time I wound my way along the coast to Cutter's Cove, I was relaxed and focused. I didn't know if I'd be able to solve the mystery of what had happened to Naomi Collins, but I was determined to try. I hoped Trevor would have news after speaking to the three people he knew because after my interview with Naomi's mother, I felt I was no further along than when I'd started.

Tucker and Sunny greeted me at the front door. I bent down to hug and kiss Tucker first. Although I'd visited often, I hadn't lived with Tucker since I'd graduated high school. I'd left him in Mom's care when I headed off to college; then, after graduation, I'd moved into a penthouse apartment in the city, while Mom had a large fenced estate. Leaving him with her had made sense. Now that we were back in the place where he'd spent his puppy years, it hit me how much I'd missed him. Sunny was a new addition to my life, one I still hadn't committed to keeping, though somehow, I knew she belonged to me as much as Tucker did. If I stayed in Cutter's Cove, I mused, I'd be able to keep both dogs. If I returned to my life in New York, I'd have to let them go. Another thing to consider as I tried to come to a firm decision about the future.

"I'm back," I sang out as I made my way up the stairs to the attic, where I found my mother painting.

Mom paused, paintbrush in her hand. "How'd it go?"

I shrugged. "I can't say I learned a lot. Naomi's mother is convinced her father loved her and would never hurt her, but I'm not so sure. I got the idea she's living in some sort of a fantasy world where her ex is a better man than he seems to be. Although I've never met him and can't with any authority make a statement regarding his level of caring for his daughter, so we'll just keep digging. I can't believe how far you've gotten on that canvas in such a short time."

Mom grinned. "I feel energized. Impassioned. I forgot how much just being here inspires me. I haven't felt this motivated to paint in a very long time."

"I'm glad you found your muse. The painting is going to be spectacular."

She turned and resumed her work. I took it as a cue to leave her to it, and went back downstairs to make some lunch. I'd just mixed up a batch of tuna salad when Trevor walked in from the drive. "Any luck?" I asked.

Trev grabbed a handful of chips. "Maybe. I have information to share. I'm just not sure how relevant it will end up being."

"Let's take these sandwiches out onto the deck. We can talk while we eat. Do you want a soda?"

"It's my day off. I'll take a beer. How'd things go with Naomi's mother?"

I spent a few minutes filling him in while we dug into the sandwiches. Then he began to tell me about his morning.

"My first stop was to Fitzgerald's Five and Dime. Naomi went to school with Donna Fitzgerald, who's now married and goes by Donna Trainer. She works for her dad, who still owns the store, and was more than happy to talk to me. According to her, Naomi was a quiet girl who never had many friends. Most of the kids at school had seen the bruises on her arms and suspected her father was physically abusive to both her and her mother. Naomi never admitted it, though, and as she got older, the bruises were commented upon less frequently. Most kids assumed Naomi had learned to stay out of the way to avoid being noticed by her father and attracting his wrath."

Trevor popped another chip into his mouth, chewed, and swallowed before he continued. "Donna did say that after her mother was sent away, Naomi began to change. She seemed to be working her way out of her shell. She even snuck out of her house a few times while her dad was away to attend parties and other social events. It was Donna's belief that after what had happened with her mother, Naomi decided to take control of her own life. She even went on a couple of dates Donna knew of. One was with Greg Dalton, which we already knew, and another was with a geeky kid who was as shy and introverted as her. Donna didn't remember his name, but everyone called him Toad."

"Did she know if Naomi had second dates with either boy?"

Trevor shook his head. "She didn't know for sure, but she didn't think so. She did say she saw Naomi in town with another guy. An older guy. She didn't know his name, but she remembered he came through town on a Harley, and somehow, Naomi got hooked up with him. He was only in town for a few days, a week at the most, and she had no idea how they met."

"Did Donna remember when it was she saw Naomi with this guy?"

"Not long before she heard Naomi was missing. She remembered wondering if Naomi hadn't come to the end of her patience with her father and took off with the guy when he left."

I tucked a lock of my blond hair behind an ear. "Did Donna tell anyone about the guy on the motorcycle? The police perhaps?"

Trevor picked up his sandwich and took a bite. "She didn't mention it to anyone. No one asked her about Naomi, and she figured if she did run away with this guy, she didn't blame her. Donna said Naomi's dad was an alcoholic and a womanizer and her mom was crazier than a loon and everyone knew it. It amazed her that Naomi hung in as long as she did."

I grabbed my phone, which contained the list I'd started. I added *guy on Harley* under the Suspects header. I had no idea how we'd figure out who this guy was sixteen years later, but just because Donna didn't know who he was didn't mean no one else did. "Did Donna have anything else interesting to say?"

"I asked her if she thought Naomi's father could have killed her and then disposed of the body. She said heck yeah. Then I asked her about Dalton, and she said that while he was a jerk in high school, he wasn't violent, and he turned out to be a nice guy. Her opinion of Mr. Kline was the most interesting."

I remembered the music teacher who some people claimed traded music lessons for sex.

Trevor went on. "Donna thought Mr. Kline was a creepy guy. She didn't take music in middle school, but she went to the school, so she knew who he was: a tall, lanky nerd who was very socially awkward. He wasn't married, and he had this way of looking at the young girls who were just developing breasts that she and others found disturbing. I asked if she thought he would have entered into a sexual relationship with Naomi if she was willing, and she thought he absolutely would have."

"Okay, we'll definitely keep him on the suspects list. Anything else from Donna?"

Trevor shook his head. He took a long sip of his beer before he started in with the results of his second interview. I sipped my water and took a look around. It was really quiet. Too quiet. It wasn't like Alyson not to be lurking around, interrupting things, especially when Trevor was here. I was pretty sure she had a crush on him, which was odd, because we were the same person and I didn't think I had a crush on him. At least, I hoped I didn't. We were friends. The last thing I wanted to do was to complicate my life more than it already was.

"Wade Stone didn't have a single nice thing to say about Naomi," Trevor said, startling me from my introspection. "The guy's a total jerk, and I'm willing to bet he was a jerk in high school too. According to him, Naomi was a nerdy geek who dressed like she lived in a Little House on the Prairie episode and was so shy she never spoke unless persuaded to by her teachers. He didn't remember a lot about her other than that he considered her to be as much a waste of air as her parents. It was his opinion that Naomi didn't have the gumption it would take to run away and start a new life, so he thinks she's dead."

"What a jerk," I said, anger coiling in my stomach.

"He really is."

"Did he suggest who might have killed her?"

"He said he didn't know, but he wouldn't be surprised if she was 'wacked by some guy she led on.' Wade thought she was a tease who'd look at a guy with big, innocent eyes that got his engine running, then cut him off if he tried to go in for a taste."

I frowned. "Sounds pretty specific. I think we should put Wade on the suspect list."

"I agree."

I had to admit I was beginning to feel irritated. Not that Naomi irritated me; I felt nothing but compassion for her. "Did you speak to the third person, John Johnson?"

"John said he didn't really know Naomi. He was in the grade ahead of her, and they didn't run in the same circles. He didn't even know who I was talking about until I found her photo in the yearbook and showed it to him."

"You have a yearbook?"

Trevor reached into his backpack and passed the book to me. The page where Naomi's photo appeared was marked. She was a pleasant-looking girl. Somewhat plain, but her large brown eyes did draw you in. She was looking straight ahead in the photo, with a very serious expression on her face. There wasn't even a trace of a smile. Her brown hair was long and straight and hung slightly over her left eye. She looked so forlorn. I could see why people had commented that she seemed to fade into the background. The blouse she wore was beige and shapeless on her thin frame, and, unlike a lot of the other girls, she wasn't wearing a speck of makeup.

"She looks as if she's just enduring," I said.

"I had the same thought."

I felt empathy grip my heart. "We need to find out what happened to her."

Trevor put his hand over mine. "We will. It might take some time, but we will."

Chapter 3

After lunch, Trevor and I decided to take a drive up the coast. He reasoned that if the bluff in my dream was a real place, and it was the location of Naomi's grave, the odds were it wouldn't be all that far from Cutter's Cove. He suggested we drive along the road for an hour in one direction, and if nothing looked familiar to me, we'd take a break and head back in the other direction. Even if we drove an hour in each direction and then backtracked, the entire trip shouldn't take more than four hours, five with short breaks. Trevor had his truck, which sported a backseat, so we took Sunny and Tucker. They'd both enjoy the ride and it would be fun to play with them on the beach when we stopped.

As we drove, I willed myself to relax. Wispy clouds floated across the deep blue sky, mimicking the color of white sails racing against the equally blue sea. "I've really missed this," I said with a sigh of contentment.

"We missed you as well," Trevor answered. "It was strange after you left. Although you'd only been in our lives for a couple of years, Mac and I felt your absence left a hole that wasn't easy to fill."

"I'm sorry I didn't make more of an effort to get back for visits. I honestly can't explain why I didn't." I turned and looked at Trevor. "It was almost like my life here was a dream. Once I got back to my old life, the time I'd spent here didn't feel real. Of course, everything came rushing back as soon as I got here. My memories. The love I felt for the sea and the people who live here."

Trevor's hands gripped the wheel as he navigated a sharp turn. "Does that mean you won't wait another ten years to come back?"

I smiled. "I'll be back so often, you'll be sick of my showing up and interrupting your life."

"You can interrupt my life anytime. Mac's too. Did you hear she decided to drive up, so she'd have her car and all her equipment? She won't be here until Thursday, but she won't have to leave so quickly, even if something comes up at work."

I brushed away the hair that had blown across my face when Trevor opened his window. "That's great. I've missed her. I can't believe she's taking three whole weeks off from her job."

"She's worked hard for a lot of years. I think she's ready for a break. The terrain begins to grow hilly after this point," Trevor said. "If you're on a bluff in your dream, there's a good chance it will be along the next fifteen or twenty miles."

"I'll keep an eye out." I squinted as I tried to bring the image from my dream into focus. In my dream, I'm standing on a bluff overlooking the sea. It wasn't a high cliff with a sharp drop like the one near the house. The land is hilly, with rises and falls weaving a fabric of peaks and valleys that all lead down to the sea. The bluff was green and grassy, with shrubs and trees that gave it color and texture. The cross was tucked behind one of those rolling hills, hidden from the beach and the main trail you'd take to get there.

"The bluffs here are too high and steep," I said after a while. "The one in my dream doesn't have a sharp drop to the sea, more of a gentle rolling of highs and lows until you gradually reach the water."

"Let's drive the full hour, then take a break. Maybe the bluff in your dreams is in the other direction." Trevor took my hand in his. "Don't worry. We'll find it."

I really hoped so. Finding the grave would at least confirm there was a murder to solve. All we knew for sure was that Naomi Collins had disappeared from Cutter's Cove sixteen years ago. What had happened to her after that was anyone's guess.

"I keep thinking about the location of the grave," I said after a while. "If it's real, and if Naomi Collins is buried there, the person who killed her must have cared about her."

Trevor frowned. "Why do you say that?"

"If some random person was responsible for her death, why would they go to all the trouble of burying her in a beautiful, peaceful spot by the sea? Why would they bother to mark the grave? The cross in my dream is generic, but if the killer was some transient passing through, why bother at all?"

"Good questions," Trevor said as the landscape began to level off again. "There's a dog-friendly beach up ahead. We'll stretch our legs before we turn around."

The narrow stretch of sand was just south of the harbor, where tall masts from boats large and small swayed from the wakes created as sailing vessels made their way along the deep-water channel that led from the shelter of the harbor to the open sea. Trevor opened the back door and allowed the dogs to jump down as a large ship with blue and white sails navigated the wide inlet toward the marina. There was something calming about a sailboat gliding across the water. I had a large painting of a sailboat on the open sea back home in my apartment. Whenever the stress from everyday life got to me, I'd look at that boat and remember my life by the sea.

"I don't think I ever visited this particular beach when I lived here," I said as Trevor tossed a stick down the long stretch of sand and sent both dogs running.

"If memory serves, we stayed pretty close to home in those days. There wasn't much of a reason to drive farther than the surfing beaches to the south of your property, and for me at least, sightseeing wasn't very interesting when I was a teenager."

"Do you enjoy it now?" I asked as we walked along the waterline. We'd left our shoes in the truck and allowed the cold water to wash over our feet.

"I do. I've actually done quite a bit of traveling during the past ten years. Road trips to one area or another. I even did a trip up into Canada a few years ago."

"Did you go alone?"

"Some of the time. Mac came along on a few of the trips. When she had time. During her college days she was pretty busy, but since she took the job in California, she's been able to get away for short stretches of time."

I paused and looked out to sea. "I'd never taken a long drive until I made the trip out here. I'm not sure why I decided to come by car; it just seemed like a good idea. And even though I didn't make stops to see anything, I enjoyed it. I've traveled a lot, but I've always flown. I had no idea how much the landscape can change from one hour to the next as you make your way across this beautiful country of ours."

"It is a pretty wonderful thing." Trevor tossed the stick again as soon as Sunny dropped it at his feet.

I laughed. "I think she has your number."

"She's a smart dog. Pretty as well, now that you have her cleaned up. When you found her, you swore you weren't going to keep her. Have you changed your mind?"

Had I? If I stayed, I'd definitely keep her, but if I returned to New York? "I'm not sure," I eventually answered. "I suppose if Mom doesn't mind keeping a second dog for me, then yeah, I'll take her with me when I leave."

Trevor didn't respond, though there was a serious look on his face. I wondered what was on his mind but didn't ask.

Once the dogs had tired themselves out, we loaded them back into the truck and started off in the other direction. While we drove, we discussed a strategy for proceeding should I not recognize the landscape in my dreams this way either but never came up with a solid plan. I tried to focus on the landscape as we doubled back through, just in case I'd missed something the first time, but my mind kept wandering to the decision I had only a few weeks to make. I supposed that wasn't completely true. If I went home to New York and then wanted to return, as long as Mom didn't sell the house, the option would still be there. I glanced over my shoulder at Sunny and Tucker. I'd missed living with the dogs.

"Is your mom planning anything for dinner?" Trevor asked.

I turned slightly in my seat. "Do you ever think about anything other than food?"

He smiled. "It wasn't that I was hinting for an invite. I just figured as long as we're heading south, we might want to stop at a café I know. It's right on the beach and they serve the best fish and chips you're likely to taste. And," Trevor added, "as a bonus, they have a dog-friendly patio. I'd enjoy sharing the place with you, but I didn't want to ruin our appetites if your mom had spent the whole day slaving over a hot stove."

"Based on the look on Mom's face as she caressed the canvas she was working on with her brush, I doubt cooking will have entered her mind. Still, it would be a good idea to text her. I'll do it right now. As long as she hasn't started dinner or made any plans, I'd love to try the place out." I glanced at the dogs behind me again. "I don't, however, think we brought leashes. Surely even a dog-friendly patio would require dogs to be leashed."

"I have a couple of leashes in my glove box," Trevor informed me.

I opened the glove box and sure as heck, Trev did have some. "Do you have a secret dog I don't know about?"

Trevor shook his head. "A woman I dated recently has two dogs. Shih Tzus. I used to help out sometimes by taking them to the vet or picking them up from the groomer. She'd always forget to send along a leash, so I started carrying a couple."

"What a nice guy you are. Do you still see her?"

"No. We gave it a go, but things didn't work out."

"I'm sorry."

Trevor shrugged. "It's for the best. We had some good times, but we didn't have a lot in common. How's your guy friend doing since you decided to stay in Cutter's Cove even though the murder you came to solve was taken care of a week ago?"

I grimaced. "He's not thrilled. Ethan is a good guy, but he doesn't understand the allure of small towns. I've tried to share my feelings about this place with him, but I'm pretty sure he thinks I'm having some sort of a breakdown. When I told him I was going to stay the full six weeks of my leave from work, he practically threatened to send his psychiatrist brother out to talk to me."

"I suppose he might just be missing you," Trevor pointed out.

"Maybe."

"Have you asked him to come here so you can share it with him?"

I laughed. "Ethan would hate everything about Cutter's Cove. Besides, I think it will work out best if I keep my life in New York and my life here separate. Somehow, I don't see the two mixing well."

Trevor didn't respond. Really, what could he say?

"So, is there anyone new in your life now that you and the Shih Tzu lady are no longer an item?" I asked.

"No. I'm totally single at the moment. Not that I really mind. I've enjoyed the time I've spent with the various women who've been part of my life, but I'm happy when I'm on my own as well."

"Really?"

Trevor shifted his visor against the sun, which had just begun to drop from its peak. "For one thing, life is less complicated when you're single. I miss the companionship, but I don't miss the drama. And I have friends, both men and women of the nonromantic sort, I can spend time with if I just want to grab a beer or bowl a few games."

"You do seem happy."

Trevor nodded. "I am. I'm even happier when you and Mac are in town."

Me too, I thought. Me too.

We were almost three quarters of the way to the café Trevor had mentioned when I spotted the bluff I'd been looking for. "There." I pointed. "That's it. I'm sure of it."

Trevor found a parking spot and we put the dogs on Trevor's leashes because we were so close to the highway. The place seemed familiar, yet I was certain I'd never been here before. In my dream, there was always fog, but now it was totally clear and sunny.

"There should be a dirt path that goes toward the sea," I said as I began to walk in the direction in which I assumed I'd find it. "We'll need to follow it until we can see the ocean from behind the lowest of the hills." I paused and thought back to my dream. "Once we can see it, we leave the path and veer to the left. A few hundred yards in and we should see the little handmade cross."

"Let's go." Trevor motioned for Tucker and me to go ahead. He followed with Sunny.

The path unfolded exactly the way it had in my dream. Rolling hills of green gave way to more rolling hills of green. The dirt path wound its way over and around the hills as it meandered toward the sea. For most of our hike, the hills blocked the view of the water, but eventually, the view opened in a sort of a V. It was at that point I knew we needed to leave the path and make our way toward the valley where I'd seen the cross.

The hike took longer in real life than it did in my dreams. I even began to doubt my instinct that this was the correct location. But other than the overall distance, everything seemed the same, so I kept walking. "There," I said just as I was about to give up. "Over that little knoll."

I hiked up and over to a small mound of earth to find the handmade wooden cross exactly as I'd seen it in my dreams. I felt tears well in my eyes as I realized the thing I feared would be true most likely was. Naomi, it seemed, hadn't gone on to have a better life after she'd left Cutter's Cove. She hadn't gone on to have any life at all.

"What do we do now?" Trevor asked.

I looked around for a sign of Naomi's spirit, which I thought might be waiting for me here. "We need to call Woody." I looked at my phone. "I don't have service."

Trevor took his own cell out of his pocket. "We need to climb up out of this valley."

I nodded, then started back the way we'd come.

******

"And there was a body in the grave?" Mom said later that evening as I shared the events of the day with her.

"There was. Woody said it was a female, but he didn't know much more than that. The body was recovered and taken to the medical examiner's office in Portland. It might be a while before we get any real news, but he promised to keep me in the loop as things unfold." Tucker wandered over and put his head in my lap. "I'm going to take the dogs out for a run before bed."

Running was one of the things that had been part of both of my lives. I'd been a runner before I'd witnessed the shooting and had to move to Cutter's Cove, and I'd continued to run after moving here. I'd run all through college, and continued to make the time to get out and hit the pavement, even after taking on my sometimes-stressful job. Running calmed my mind. It helped me focus. There was something about the rhythm of my own feet hitting the ground that helped me reboot and recharge. Anytime I had a big decision to make, I took to the streets. A difficult day at work meant a run through the park. Running, I realized, was another one of the things about me that Ethan didn't approve of. He'd tried on numerous occasions to get me to join his gym. He'd argued that it was safer, drier when the weather was bad, and a lot seemlier than logging miles in the park or on the street. But I didn't want to work out in a room filled with boring machines, which might very well make you sweat but would never feed your soul. For me, running wasn't about burning calories or raising my heart rate; it was about being immersed in the world, being part of the colors, scents, weather, and noise that defined who we were and where we chose to spend our time.

Finding a pace that suited both Sunny the puppy and Tucker the senior was tricky, but after a few starts and stops, I found one that was comfortable for Tucker and let Sunny run back and forth, logging extra miles as she ran ahead, then turned and circled back. Like the day had been, the night was breathtaking. The clear sky displayed millions of twinkling stars that were so much brighter here by the dark sea than they were at home, where skyscrapers blocked them and the city lights drowned them out. The moon had yet to make an appearance, so the night was dark. I watched the ground ahead of me as the light from the small flashlights I wore on each arm showed the way.

The roar of the waves breaking on the rocks at the foot of the bluff informed me that it was high tide, or close to it. I let my mind drift back to Cutter's Cove ten years ago. Tucker and I had jogged along this hardpacked dirt path on more occasions than I could count. I had very vivid memories of my time in here now that I was back, which made me wonder why I'd forgotten it so completely while I was away.

I thought about my life in New York. If I was home, I'd probably have worked late, then been too tired to go for a run after I'd gotten home. That would have suited Ethan just fine. We'd have a drink, talk about our days, then be too exhausted to remember what passion felt like. As I ran through the night, I wondered how we'd gotten to this point. I guess one day at a time, each leading us farther from the attraction we'd felt when we first met, but both too preoccupied to notice or care. Whether I stayed or went back, I knew my relationship with Ethan had come to its logical conclusion. I hated to break up over the phone, but I hated to wait. Maybe I could try to set up a Skype session for tomorrow night.

I wondered if Ethan would be hurt, then realized that once he'd had a minute to think about it, like me, he probably wouldn't care. Everyone who knew us said we were well suited, but if I were honest with myself, even in the beginning I knew we never were. Not that we didn't share moments of passion. It was just that the passion had given way to an easy companionship sooner than it should have.

I paused and called Sunny back. She could probably run for hours, but it was late, and I was tired. Today had been both productive and difficult. I'd set out to find the grave in my dreams, and I had. Yet there had been a part of me that didn't want to prove Naomi Collins was dead. Not that finding the grave proved the body inside it was Naomi's, but deep in my soul I knew it did.

Yes, today had been a challenge, but tomorrow would be another day. I'd follow the leads Trevor and I had turned up and then, on Thursday, Mac would be here and everyone I considered to be family would be together in one place for the first time in a very long time.

Chapter 4

Tuesday, June 12

The following morning, I did what I'd done almost every morning since I'd been back. I made a cup of coffee and took it out onto the deck. Today, the clouds on the horizon were heavy, so I doubted we'd enjoy the colorful display we had the day before. Tucker and Sunny lay on the deck near the chair where I sat while Shadow took up residence on one of the padded loungers. The sea was rougher this morning than it usually was, indicating to me that a storm might be on the way.

I took a sip from my blue ceramic mug as I let the morning sooth me. When Mom and I had remodeled the house, she had decided to decorate using the colors from the sea. The rooms varied one from the others somewhat, but the whole house displayed shades of blue, gray, white, and beige. There was some black thrown in for contrast, but overall, it had a feel I found perfect for the location.

"Did you call him?" Alyson popped in from out of nowhere and sat down on the chair next to me.

"Call who?"

"Ethan. Last night when we were running, you thought about calling Ethan. You thought about ending things with him. You thought about how he no longer filled a space in your life."

I glared at Alyson. "It freaks me out that you can read my thoughts."

"*Our* thoughts."

"If my thoughts really are *our* thoughts, you should know whether I called Ethan."

"I know you didn't call him. I was trying to tactfully suggest you do it by asking if you had. And soon. Before you change your mind."

"Our mind." I smiled.

Alyson giggled. "Fine. Our mind. You know he doesn't fit into our life like he once might have."

I lifted a brow. "Do you remember my life in New York even though you weren't there and we weren't merged?"

Alyson shook her head. "Not really. If you remember something now during the time we're merged, I can experience that memory."

"You're freaking me out again, this merging only to separate again. Having you rattling around in my thoughts and memories."

"*Our* thoughts and memories," Alyson corrected.

"Whatever. Any way you slice it, it's disturbing. First thing today I'm heading in to town to talk to Chan."

Alyson shrugged. "Suit yourself, but you know what he's going to say."

"I do?"

"We know I exist in form as a representation of the parts of you that you left behind in Cutter's Cove. Chan will tell you that we're beginning to merge for periods of time because you're beginning to accept those parts back into your life. We also know he'll tell you assimilation won't and can't be complete until you commit to staying here. If you do stay, you might not have to deal with me chatting you up like this."

Alyson was right. That was exactly what Chan would say.

"So how about it?" she asked. "We both know you're thinking about it. Staying, that is. Are you going to?"

I let out a breath. "I have been thinking about it. But it's an important decision that shouldn't be hurried."

Alyson curled her legs under herself. "Maybe, but either way, we're over Ethan. Call him."

"I will."

"You will what?" Mom asked as she came out onto the deck with her own cup of coffee. She sat down on the chair Alyson had vacated when she disappeared as abruptly as she'd appeared.

"I've come to a decision, and I guess I was just confirming it to myself."

"What decision, if you don't mind me asking?"

I took a deep breath. "I've decided to end things with Ethan. I was going to wait until I got home, but I think I'm going to call him from here. It seems wrong to keep him hanging now that I've made up my mind."

Mom blew on her coffee, then took a sip. "I'm not surprised. In fact, I'm sort of surprised you hung on as long as you did."

"Really? Was it that obvious?"

Mom shrugged. "Maybe not to others, but I'm your mother. I know you. I could see the two of you weren't suited. I've wanted to say something for a while, but I made a vow a long time ago not to be one of those mothers who meddles in their daughters' lives."

I let out a breath that was almost a laugh. "If you'd said something, I'm sure I wouldn't have listened. I seem to have inherited your stubborn, independent streak."

Mom laughed out loud. "That, my love, is putting it mildly. Still, while I'm sorry Booker was murdered, I'm glad you had a reason to return to Cutter's Cove. It seems as if the trip has helped you gain some perspective."

I nodded. "It has." I paused. "There's something else. While nothing's set in stone yet, I've been thinking about staying. Permanently," I emphasized.

"Again, I'm not surprised. When I got here and realized how happy you are, I pretty much assumed you would."

I reached over and hugged Mom. "I should have known you would know what was going on in my head. You always could read me."

"Again, I'm your mother. There are things a mother knows about her child."

"If I do stay, I'd like to keep the house."

"I've been hanging on to this place for ten years because somewhere in the back of my mind I knew this was where you'd ultimately end up."

I lifted a brow. "You knew I'd come back?"

Mom nodded. "I did. I just didn't know it would take so long. The house is and always has been your home. I knew you and the house were connected the moment we first saw it. We looked at dozens of others, all better suited to a single woman and her teenage daughter, but when you set eyes on this dilapidated old house that looked as if a strong wind could blow it over, I knew we were home."

I felt a tear slide down my cheek. Emotion gripped me as I remembered that moment. "Everyone thought we were crazy. Not only was this house a total wreck but everyone said it was haunted. And, as it turned out, it was. But in a good way. In a life-affirming way. Not in an Amityville Horror way."

Mom reached out and tucked my straight blond hair behind my ear. "I knew the moment you were born that you were going to be exceptional. And you were, from the beginning. But when I saw you face the death of your best friend, witness protection, and a move across the country with grace and acceptance, I knew *exceptional* was much too mild a word for my amazing daughter. You have something special. Something no one else has. While I'll miss you if you stay, I really do think for you to reach your ultimate potential, your destiny is here."

"If I stay, you'll come and visit?"

Mom hugged me. "All the time. So often you might wish I'd stay away."

"Never. This is your home too. Your room will always be your room, and you're welcome to spend as much time as you want here. In fact, if you ever grow tired of New York, you're welcome to stay here with me forever."

Mom laughed. "I'm sure your future husband would love that."

"I'd never marry a man who wouldn't love having you in our lives," I replied in all seriousness.

Mom put a hand over mine. "It sounds like you've come to your decision."

I felt a huge weight lift. "Yes. I think I have."

******

Later that morning, I called Ethan. I still felt bad about sharing my news over the phone, but now that I was sure, I knew I couldn't wait. As I expected, he seemed fine with it. In fact, he seemed relieved. We made arrangements for him to ship the things I'd kept at his apartment, and we promised to keep in touch, but I knew we wouldn't.

The call to my boss was a bit harder. I was a valuable asset to the advertising agency I worked for, and I knew they'd miss my unique designs. In the beginning, the conversation was rocky, but when I offered to continue to create designs and ad campaigns for them as a freelance artist, we were able to end it on a much more positive note.

As an heiress to old money and a lot of it, I didn't need to work, but that didn't mean I didn't want to. The more I thought about it, the surer I was that starting my own photo and design business was exactly what I wanted to do. The attic was large enough so Mom could keep a space for her painting while I had room for my own studio. I'd need space for computers, design and matting boards, but that wouldn't be an issue.

Filled with more enthusiasm than I'd experienced in a long time, I told Mom I was going into town, then headed to the police station. I figured Woody must know something by now about the body buried on the bluff, and the only thing that could make this day even more perfect would be to solve the mystery of my dreams.

"Morning, Woody," I said as I walked into his office without bothering to knock on the open door and took a seat across the desk from him.

"I thought you might be by today, but I didn't expect you to be in such a good mood. You're glowing. Do you know something I don't? Because the only news I have is bad."

"I am in a good mood, but it has nothing to do with Naomi Collins. You said you have news?"

Woody nodded. "We found a necklace around the neck of the skeleton and described it to Mrs. Landry, who confirmed it belonged to her daughter. The medical examiner is still working on a timeline, but it's his belief that she's probably been there ever since she disappeared."

My smile faded just a bit. "I had a feeling. Still, I'm really sorry to hear it. Do you have an idea about the cause of death?"

"It looks like blunt force trauma to the head. There's a mark on one of her ribs that could have been broken, but the ME is going with the head injury."

I took a deep breath and held it for a moment, focusing on the pressure in my lungs rather than the rattling in my brain. Now that I knew it was Naomi's grave in my dreams, I was certain I was meant to find out who'd put her in the ground near the sea. "Do you have any working theories about who might have killed her?"

"Other than the suspects Officer Young identified, not really. I kind of hoped you might have found something."

"I have a short list of potential suspects. Some we can easily follow up on, others may be out of our reach. I'm committed to working on this until the case is solved. I assume that now that you have a body you are as well."

Woody nodded. "Absolutely. There's a whiteboard in the conference room in the back. I'll let them know up front not to disturb us." Woody paused and looked at me. "I'm happy for your help, but are you sure this is how you want to spend the rest of your vacation?"

"I'm no longer on vacation," I informed him. "As of nine a.m. Pacific Standard Time, I officially quit my job."

Woody frowned. "You quit your job? Why?"

"I'm staying in Cutter's Cove."

Woody raised a brow. "You're staying here? Permanently?"

I nodded. "But don't say anything to anyone yet. I still need to tell Trev and Mac."

Woody's face broke into a huge grin. "Well, welcome, neighbor. I'm happy you decided to come back."

"Not as happy as I am."

******

It took us over two hours, but after batting names back and forth, Woody and I came up with a list of suspects, as well as a list of people to interview. The suspects included four people we both had on our lists, three people on my list only, and three people only on Woody's. From the shared list, we had Naomi's father, Bodine Collins; the music teacher, Jeffrey Kline; the transient seen talking to Naomi, Frank Joplin; and Greg Dalton, Naomi's date shortly before she went missing. Thanks mostly to Trevor's efforts, I had the guy on the Harley, who Donna had seen with Naomi; Wade Stone, the classmate who considered Naomi a tease; and Toad, the nerdy kid it was believed she'd also dated. Woody had a man named Ron Pullman, who had been doing some handyman work on the house next to the Collins place and was now a registered sex offender; Carl Woodbine, the husband of the woman Bodine Collins had been sleeping with, who, Woody theorized, might have come by the house to confront her father only to find him gone and killed Naomi either in rage or as a means of revenge; and Peter Steadman, who was the janitor at the high school when Naomi was a student, who was later fired for spying on students in the girls' locker room.

"So, who's around and who's long gone?" I asked.

Woody ran his eye over the board. "Bodine Collins is still living in Cutter's Cove, as is Greg Dalton and Wade Stone. And Carl Woodbine and Peter Steadman are both around. We have no way of knowing where the guy on the Harley or Toad are unless we can identify them by name. Frank Joplin moved on and Jeffrey Kline left the area shortly after Naomi disappeared, though he isn't that far away."

"How about Ron Pullman?" I asked.

"I'm not sure," Woody answered. "I'll see what I can find out."

I stood back and looked at the board. "It's not going to be easy to figure this out. It's been so long, and a lot of our suspects are gone." I stared a bit longer. "My instinct is that the killer won't be the guy working next door or the homeless man. Naomi's grave was really lovely. And it was marked. To me, that speaks of a killer who knew her. Who cared about her."

"Like her father," Woody said.

I nodded. "Or the music teacher, who'd known her since middle school. My gut is telling me the killer will turn out to be one of them. Or, perhaps, someone else who knew and cared for her and hasn't yet made it to this board. She didn't have any siblings and her mother was in the mental health facility when Naomi's disappeared. So far, I haven't found any close friends. Did she have grandparents? Aunts or uncles? Cousins?"

"According to the report left by Officer Young, Naomi's paternal grandparents were dead, and her maternal grandparents lived in South Carolina. It seems they more or less disowned their daughter when she married Bodine Collins, so Naomi had never even met them. Mrs. Collins was an only child. Her husband had a brother, Chester, and a half sister, Eleanor. Chester lived in Kansas at the time of Naomi's disappearance and Eleanor was the product of his father's second marriage and was never part of his life. Officer Young didn't think a relative from either side was involved in Naomi's life before or after she disappeared."

"I wonder why Mr. Collins told Officer Young that Naomi didn't have an aunt pregnant or otherwise when he inquired about her absence from school."

Woody shrugged. "I suppose because Eleanor wasn't his mother's child."

"I guess that makes sense." I glanced at the board again, then looked back at Woody.

"I suppose it wouldn't hurt to contact Eleanor and Chester to see if they have anything to say."

"Couldn't hurt," I agreed.

Woody crossed his arms over his chest as he studied the board. He'd filled out since I'd first met him ten years ago, when he was a brand-new cop, as green as they come. He struck me then and now as being someone who gave a damn, which I liked, and he hadn't been hardened the way a lot of cops who'd been on the force for a long time became. He was almost always willing to think outside the box, and to listen to what I had to say. I remembered feeling an immediate attraction to him when I first met him, even though I was only seventeen and he was twenty-one. To a seventeen-year-old girl, a man in uniform with thick brown hair that waved down to his collarbone, eyes the color of rich hickory, and a body as honed as any man coming out of the service was likely to be, was pretty darn appealing.

"So, other than contacting these long-lost relatives, what do we do at this point?" I asked after a bit.

"I guess we keep digging."

I nodded. Of course, the best way to find out who'd killed Naomi was to ask her. She hadn't been present when we'd found her body, so I wondered if she had already moved on. But if she had, why had I been having the dreams in the first place?

Chapter 5

I left the police station and went to Pirates Pizza. I wanted to be sure Trevor remained part of the process every step of the way. When I'd lived here before, I'd shared my huge secret about being in the witness protection program because of the men who were after me with Mac but not with Trevor. I hadn't meant to slight him. Mac had found out by accident, and I wasn't supposed to tell anyone. When Trevor eventually found out, it was obvious I'd hurt him deeply. I wasn't sure he'd completely forgiven me.

"Guess what I did this morning?" I asked him after sliding into a red vinyl booth at the front of the restaurant.

"Solved the murder."

"Unfortunately, I think we're a long way away from doing that. I just saw Woody, and I do have news, but it can wait for a bit. I have bigger news of a personal nature."

Trevor raised a brow. The little gleam in his eye gave away exactly what he was thinking. "A personal nature?"

I hit his arm. "Not that personal."

Trevor slid into the booth across from me. He leaned forward, giving me his full attention. "Okay, what did you do this morning?"

I grinned with satisfaction. "I broke up with my boyfriend and quit my job."

Trevor looked confused. "Quit your job?"

"Actually," I corrected, "I *tried* to quit my job, but they wouldn't let me, so I worked out a deal to work as a freelancer."

A look of delight mingled with caution came over Trevor's face. "You're staying?"

I nodded. "I'm staying."

I'm not sure how we got from sitting in the booth across from each other to him holding me in his arms and twirling me around the room, but the next thing I knew, I was being twirled. And what a ride it was. I felt as happy as a child on Christmas morning as I tried to focus on a spot on the wall to keep from getting dizzy. It had been a long time since my joy had been so complete.

"You aren't teasing?" Trevor asked after he stopped twirling. "Please tell me this isn't some sort of a joke."

"I'm not teasing," I assured him as I gripped his arm so I wouldn't fall flat on my butt. "I talked to Mom, and she's fine with me staying in the house. I talked to my boss, who's fine with me working freelance. And I broke up with Ethan, who didn't seem upset about me ending things. I'm really, really staying."

Trevor pulled me close and kissed me on the lips. It was a brief, friendly sort of kiss, but it still managed to send a whirling tingling through my core and down my legs.

"We have to call Mac," Trevor said.

"No."

"No?" Trev asked.

"She'll be here in a couple of days, I want to tell her in person. Let's just keep this between us for now."

Trevor nodded. "Okay, if that's what you want. I think this calls for a celebration. I have to work this evening, but I close early during the week. Come by at eight and I'll make you something special."

"Okay." I hugged Trevor again. "In the meantime, I have a ghost to hunt down."

******

I headed back to the grave after I left Trevor. If I could contact Naomi's spirit, she might be able to help me explain her death, as Booker had in the last murder I'd helped to solve. If she hadn't moved on, if she was trapped somewhere, either at the grave or in the house where she'd lived at the time she disappeared, I had a good chance of connecting with her. While I'd seen quite a few ghosts during my time in Cutter's Cove as a teenager, I wasn't certain how each one chose the location where they stayed while they waited for the help they needed to move on.

Barkley Cutter, the first ghost I'd ever happened upon, had lived and died in the house Mom and I bought. After his death, he'd waited to move on until he was able to share the secret that bound him to the earthly plane. For reasons unknown to me, most likely proximity, I was the one he reached out to. Mac, Trevor, some other friends, and I were able to give him the closure he needed. After that, I'd developed the ability to see other ghosts. Not all ghosts, and not all the time. It wasn't as if I walked around seeing dead people everywhere. It was more as if I could see spirits who, for reasons of their own, allowed me to connect with them.

While I'd helped several ghosts while I lived in Cutter's Cove, the power hadn't come with me to New York. When I'd returned to Cutter's Cove this summer, I was delighted to find my gift had returned. Booker had been a close friend years ago, so our connection made sense. I just hoped I could help Naomi find her closure as well.

At the grassy bluff overlooking the sea, I found a large rock to sit on near the spot where Naomi had been buried. I looked out toward the sea of endless blue, the sky darkened by the approaching clouds that threated a storm. The breeze was gentle, although the promise of a stronger gale could be seen on the choppy water beyond the wave break. I relaxed and allowed images and voices to filter through. If Naomi was nearby, I wanted to have an open mind and heart to accept her presence.

"Don't forget to pull your hair back before Papa gets home," a shrill reminder filtered through my mind. The voice was more of an echo from the past than a directive from the present, and I knew the voice wasn't an echo from my own life. "You know how your papa gets when your hair hangs over your eyes."

"Yes, Mama," the girl sighed. She put a hand to her cheek as she considered her large brown eyes and colorless face in the mirror. She wondered what it would be like to wear makeup, have her hair styled, and wear clothes that weren't two sizes too big for her. She wondered what it would be like to dress in a way that would get her noticed. Papa wouldn't like it. Good girls didn't call attention to themselves. She obeyed so as not to incur his wrath, but in the silent moments, when she was alone with her thoughts, she wondered.

"There's a dance at school next week," she said, an edge of caution in her voice.

"You know how your father feels about dancing."

Her heart fluttered as she considered her response. "I do. But Papa has that fishing trip. I thought maybe he wouldn't have to know."

Her mother looked at her. I could feel disappointment in my mind. "Good girls don't lie to their fathers. Besides, you have nothing to wear."

That was true. She was a plain girl who wore boring clothes from the secondhand store. It made no sense for her to dream about pretty dresses and swaying to music in the arms of the man of her dreams.

"I think you're beautiful," I thought, in an attempt to break into the memory that had to be Naomi's, to make a connection in my mind. "Quite remarkable." I waited, but the voices had faded. "I want to be your friend," I tried, but the voices remained silent. "I want to help you."

I waited quietly until I heard a tiny whisper so faint I was sure I'd imagined it. "Papa wouldn't like it."

"We don't have to tell him," I assured the girl in my mind.

"I can't. Good girls don't lie." And she was gone, her voice silent.

I opened my eyes. It seemed making a connection with Naomi was going to be difficult. She hadn't actually appeared on an earthly plane. At least not when I was around. I wondered if she ever would.

Still, a gentle whisper in my mind was better than nothing at all. I'd just keep trying. Eventually, I hoped, she would come to trust me.

I looked out at the dark, heavy clouds that had been hanging offshore all day but were beginning to roll inland. I could hear the rumble of thunder as the wind picked up and the sea grew rougher. I'd need to come back another day. Perhaps tomorrow. I found myself wishing Alyson was here. It occurred to me that a sixteen-year-old apparition might be more apt to connect with the sixteen-year-old part of me.

When I'd first stumbled upon Alyson, I'd been freaked out, then annoyed. Yet I was learning to love her. That must mean I was learning to love the part of myself she represented. She had a purity and compassion I'd lost as Amanda. Perhaps by finding a way to join myself, I wouldn't simply be eliminating a pest but would be reclaiming some of the best of me, the parts I seemed to have lost along the way. My decision to stay in Cutter's Cove most likely meant we'd be reunited as a whole. I wondered if I'd ever see her again. Part of me understood that integration was vital. Another understood I'd miss the insanity of the whole thing.

"I'm going now," I said out loud, in the event Naomi was lingering. "I know you're frightened. I'd be frightened too. I want to help you. I think I can." I paused and looked out at the quickly approaching storm. "There's a storm coming. I'll be back tomorrow if I can." I stood up and looked at the taped-off area where the grave had been. "I'm sorry."

With that, I returned to my car. As I was driving home it occurred to me that I should turn in my Mercedes sedan for something a bit more practical. I had two dogs to cart around now; something with a cargo area would work a lot better than loading and unloading them into the backseat. I knew there was a Mercedes dealer in Portland, only a couple of hours away. Maybe I'd pop over and look at some four-wheel-drive SUVs.

******

"Amanda, how nice to see you," Chan greeted me as I entered his shop filled with everything magic. "I hoped you'd stop by."

I picked up a jar of newt eyes, grimaced, and then set it back on the shelf with other strange and wonderful objects. "You always seem to know everything, so I assume you already know I've decided to stay."

Chan nodded. "It was your destiny."

I wandered around the shop, picking up and putting down books, tarot cards, and scented candles. "I believe it too. And I'm happy with my decision. Thrilled, actually." I set the candle I'd been holding back on its shelf. "I'm here to ask you about Alyson. Now that I've committed to staying, will we be one again?"

"Do you feel her essence?"

I nodded. "I do. Not only am I happier than I've been since I was a teenager, but I can feel the childlike energy I seemed to have left behind at some point. I guess I can assume that energy comes from Alyson, but it feels odd to me that she's just gone. How do I know for certain she's with me? How do I know she's okay?"

Chan came around from behind the counter and took my hand in his. Then he closed his eyes. I took several deep breaths as I waited for him to speak.

"I sense that the fracture in your life force has been repaired," Chan said in his matter-of-fact way. "I sense unity and strength."

"So Alyson is back on the inside?"

"I believe so."

"Will she stay there?"

"That, my friend, is up to you."

I frowned. "Up to me? I don't understand. How is it up to me?"

Chan went to the back of the store, straightening items as he did. I followed as he set a pace I knew would match the unhurried tempo of his life. Eventually, he spoke. "The fragmentation of your psyche occurred when you left behind the part of yourself you felt would not be congruent with your life in New York. The childlike part. The part that believed in magic. Now that you have committed to a life in Cutter's Cove, you have accepted the magic, and the fragmentation has been made whole. Alyson isn't gone. She has always been a part of you. Now she lives through you, as she once did."

I let out a groan. "I'm not sure I understand this. I want to, but it's too abstract."

Chan handed me a crystal ball. "Consider this. You can hold it in your hands. It is solid and whole, a single entity made up of a specific amount of energy. Now, imagine cutting the ball in half. The whole is now made up of two pieces, yet nothing has been lost. The energy contained in the whole still exists. It is just fragmented."

"Okay. That makes sense, I guess."

"Now suppose you heat the glass so you can meld the two pieces back together. The two exist as a single entity again, yet at no point was anything lost or gained."

I narrowed my eyes as I let that sink in. "I guess your analogy works. It's the same as if you have a glass of water. You can pour half of it into another glass, but the total volume of water stays the same. It feels a lot different when it comes to a person being fragmented or whole, but I guess I get it." I looked at Chan. "I'll miss her."

"You cannot miss what isn't actually gone. I can teach you how to channel your consciousness, but that will be a lesson for another day."

I stepped forward and hugged Chan. "Thank you for everything. I would like to learn how to channel my consciousness, but I agree it's something for another day. Today, I have an SUV to buy."

******

"You got a new car," Mom said later that afternoon when I got back from Portland.

I ran a hand over the black Mercedes GLS 550. Boy, she was pretty. I didn't usually go all gaga over a new vehicle, but this one spoke to me. "I figured if I was staying in Cutter's Cove, I needed something better suited to hauling dogs, surfboards, and home repair supplies. My sedan was great, but this," I leaned onto the hood and gave it a hug, "this is perfect for my new life."

"It's beautiful. And practical. I love it."

I grinned. "I can't wait to take her off road. Maybe down to the beach. Do you want to take a ride?"

"I'd love to take a ride, but I'm in the middle of a canvas. I have open paint and I need to get back. But I want a ride later. Maybe we could head down the coast."

"I'd love that, but I can't tonight." I wiped a speck of dust from the shiny hood. "I'm heading into town to meet Trevor. I was just going to let you know I wouldn't be here for dinner."

"That's probably just as well," Mom answered. "I'm on a roll with my latest creation and will probably be working late into the night. I wouldn't be taking a break even now, but I happened to be looking out the window when you drove up." Mom paused and took a step forward. She put a hand on my arm. "It's good to see you so happy."

Mom returned to the attic and I headed inside to put away a few groceries I'd stopped to pick up. Tucker and Sunny both came running up, tails wagging, bodies wiggling with joy. There was one thing that could be said for having a dog or two: Every time you walked in the door, you were greeted by someone who loved you.

As I put the groceries away, I glanced around the kitchen. Mom loved to cook, and she'd gone all out when she remodeled this room. She'd had it taken down to the studs, then completely rebuilt. New windows overlooking the sea, new countertops, cabinets, and floors. The colors she'd chosen were restful. Peaceful, in a way. Mom had wanted to bring the feel of the sea indoors while maintaining the country feel of the large room. In addition to the grays, blues, and whites utilized throughout, she'd integrated the distressed brick of the old fireplace, with colorful accents throughout.

Now that I'd decided to stay, and the house would be mine, I planned to add a few new touches. Mom had bought restaurant-grade appliances and used quality materials, so, other than a fern for the kitchen nook, a garden window for the herbs I planned to plant, and a few dark gray dishes to mix in with the white and cobalt blue, the room would be perfect for me.

The hardwood floors throughout the first story were rich and polished to reflect the light. I loved the floors, but I found I wasn't a huge fan of the fussy area rug Mom had chosen for the living area. Replacing the rug with something more to my taste would be my first action as a homeowner. Or perhaps home borrower was more accurate. Mom's name was still, after all, on the deed. Maybe we could remedy that as well.

I took the dogs out for a run. It had started to sprinkle just a bit, but it wasn't too bad yet. The dogs didn't seem to care about the moisture in the air, and I was so happy, I didn't either. I found my mind racing a million miles a minute as I thought about everything I wanted to do in the next few days. Of course, finding out exactly what had happened to Naomi would be a priority. It was true she'd been dead for sixteen years, so any true urgency most likely only existed in my mind. Still, I'd been having the dreams for some time, and quieting them so I could get the rest I needed was important.

I was excited to dig in and start making the house feel more like my own, but new rugs and accents could wait. I'd had a crew in to take care of the heavy cleaning when I'd first arrived, so other than the yard, which looked kind of sad, the house was perfectly livable for the time being.

After we'd covered a couple of miles, I called the dogs back and headed home. I wanted to shower and dress for my dinner with Trevor. As I neared the house, I wished Mac was here. I wasn't sure why exactly, because Trevor and I had been friends since we were kids, but it almost felt like our dinner tonight was a date. That thought in and of itself was odd; he and I had shared many meals with just the two of us. I thought of Alyson and her teenage hormones and wondered if the date vibe wasn't coming from her.

I took my time with my rain-scented shampoo, conditioner, and body wash, then dried my hair so it hung loose down my back. Then I applied a very light touch of makeup and went into the bedroom to decide what to wear.

Trevor owned a pizza parlor, so I assumed he planned to cook me something to eat in its kitchen, probably pizza. That would be a casual sort of meal, although it would be the first time Trev had cooked anything for me, and that meant something. While dressy attire might not be appropriate, shorts and a tank might be a bit too casual. Slipping into a sunny yellow sundress, I slid my feet into white sandals, and grabbed a white sweater just in case it grew chilly once the sun set. I tossed in a raincoat as well just in case. I called upstairs to let Mom know I was leaving, said goodbye to the animals, and headed out to my terrific new SUV.

Chapter 6

The storm had blown in big-time while I'd been getting ready. I'd actually expected it earlier. As with most summer rains here, the air was warm and the humidity high. It had been dry since I'd been in town, so the area could probably benefit from a heavy downpour. I just hoped the worst of it would wait until I got home. Trevor was just turning the Open sign to Closed when I pulled up in front of Pirates Pizza. He waved at me, pulled a slicker over his head, and jogged out onto the sidewalk and to my SUV.

"You got it!" He poked his head in through the window I'd lowered when I saw him come out.

I nodded. "Better for hauling dogs and surfboards, right? A must now that I'm staying."

"It's gorgeous. A bit out of my price range, but gorgeous."

"Thanks. I like it."

"The big cargo area will come in handy. I rode my bike into work today." Trev looked up to the dark sky and steady rain. "I didn't anticipate the rain, although I should have, given the dark clouds on the horizon this morning. Maybe you and your SUV can give me and my bike a ride home?"

"I'd be happy to. Do you want to eat first?"

Trevor shook his head. "I'm going to cook for you in my own recently remodeled kitchen. I would have had you meet me at my place if you knew where it was. Hang on. I'll finish locking up, grab my bike, and come back out."

"Do you need help?" I asked.

"No reason for you to get soaked. I'll only be a minute."

I frowned as Trevor walked away. I'd anticipated a casual dinner in the restaurant; somehow dining with Trevor in his apartment seemed too intimate. I wondered why that worried me. I recited the mantra I seemed to have had in mind most of the day: Trev and I are old friends; good friends. Dining alone with him in his apartment shouldn't be any more intimate than dining with Mac in hers would be. Taking a deep breath, I assured myself that any nerves I might be feeling were the result of there being so many recent adventures in my life. It was natural to be tense in these situations; the butterflies in my stomach had nothing to do with the evening ahead.

I glanced out the windshield at the intensifying rain. Trevor had mentioned his remodeled kitchen, and that confused me. We hadn't discussed his living space except in passing, but I'd pictured him living in one of the cookie-cutter apartments in town. I remembered when I'd asked about his apartment and he'd said it was nice, but was it remodeled-kitchen nice? I tried to bring back the whole conversation.

He'd said he had a place by the beach. There were a ton of condos and apartment buildings there. Some were rundown and dingy, while others were newly built. If it was nice, I pictured a newer building. But a remodeled kitchen didn't fit any image I could call up.

I turned as Trevor jogged through the now-steady rain with his bike. He opened the SUV tailgate, slipped his bike into the cargo area, then came around to the passenger side door. Inside, he told me to take Main to the coast road. When he directed me to a small house directly on the sand, I was both awed and surprised.

"I thought you said you lived in an apartment," I said as I pulled into the drive.

"I never said I lived in an apartment. You asked me about my place and I said it was nice. If you imagined it was an apartment, that's all you."

I supposed Trev had a point. I guess I just assumed a single guy in his late twenties would live in an apartment. "You own this house?"

"All sixteen hundred square feet of it."

I turned off the ignition. "Wow. I'm impressed. I can't wait to see it."

"It was a total wreck when I bought it, which was the only reason I could afford it, but I've been fixing it up a little at a time. It's taken some elbow grease for sure, but I think I have it just about where I want it."

Trevor unloaded his bike while I hurried through the rain to the front deck. Trev leaned the bike against a wall, then pulled out a key to open the front door. The interior of the house was open and spacious. In my experience, sixteen hundred wasn't a lot of square feet; the entire first floor was one large space, opening up to both the kitchen and the dining area. The view out the double sliding doors was amazing. I mean, really amazing. The view from the house on the bluff was pretty spectacular, but being able to walk out your back door onto the sand…wow!

"I can't believe you live here," I said as I walked across the dark tile of the entire first floor.

"You've been picturing me living in a dumpy apartment."

"Well, yeah," I said, amazement still evident in my voice.

"Why?" Trevor asked.

I paused. Then frowned. "I have no idea. You do have your own business, and you drive a nice truck. I should have assumed you'd have a nice place. But this? Well, this… I mean, look at that kitchen. Can you actually cook?"

Trevor laughed. "Of course I can cook. I own a restaurant."

"You own a pizza parlor. Not the same thing," I countered as I crossed the room to look out at the darkening sky and steady waves.

"Have you bothered to look at the menu of my little pizza parlor?"

I narrowed my gaze on him. "No, I guess not. I assumed it was the same menu Pirates Pizza always had."

Trevor came over to stand next to me. He smelled good. Male and earthy, not at all like the strong cologne Ethan wore. "If you'd taken the time to look at the menu, you would have seen that in addition to pizza, I serve a variety of pasta dishes, as well as Italian specialties like eggplant parmigiana."

I frowned again. In fact, I had been frowning so much since I'd arrived at Trevor's awesome house that if my grandmother were here, she'd be cautioning me that my face was going to freeze that way. "Where did you learn to make eggplant parmigiana?"

"I've been taking classes, as well as doing some online tutorials. When I bought Pirates Pizza, I decided I wanted to serve more than just pizza, so I hired a chef and learned how to cook."

The fact that I had no idea Trevor had been taking cooking classes made me feel really bad. "I'm sorry. I should have known that."

Trev shrugged. "It's not important now. Would you like some wine?"

"I'd love some."

Trevor's taste in wine was as pleasant a surprise as his little beach house. I took a sip and let it linger on my tongue before swallowing. "This is very good."

"Local vintner. It'll take me about thirty minutes to throw dinner together. You can sit at the bar and watch if you'd like, or if you prefer, have a seat in the living area."

"I'll watch," I decided. "I can't wait to see what you can do."

What Trevor could do, I soon learned, was surprising. And amazing. And kind of a turn-on. I'd always loved a man who could cook. Not that I knew many. But there had been a few over the years, and watching strong hands covered in dark hair as they sliced and diced, whipped and stirred, felt primal and sensual. Trevor didn't take shortcuts by using anything that was prepackaged, -shredded, or -

chopped. His choice of main course for the evening was a scampi dish made with plump prawns, asparagus, a lemon butter sauce, and fresh herbs. The scampi was going to be served, I was informed, over what looked to be homemade pasta.

"Can I help?" I asked after I'd watched for a while.

"I have garlic bread ready to go into the oven, but I didn't have time to toss together a salad. Everything is in the crisper if you want to assemble one."

I slid off the stool. "I'd be happy to."

Trev handed me a wooden salad bowl that looked handmade. The sort of thing you'd buy in an expensive boutique. Who was this sophisticated and accomplished adult I was dining with, and what had he done with the man-child I remembered?

When I looked into the crisper, I found a variety of greens and vegetables all washed and individually packaged. I selected several items I thought would complement each other.

"There's a homemade dressing in the red Tupperware and fresh parmesan to shred for the top. If you need anything you aren't finding, just holler."

"Do you cook like this every night?" I asked as I assembled the salad.

Trevor laughed. "No. Most nights I eat at the restaurant or make a sandwich. I do like to make an actual meal, though, when I have the time, which lately hasn't been all that often."

I paused to just look at him. I was pretty sure my mouth was hanging open.

"You seem surprised by all this," he said.

"More like amazed. You do like to eat more than anyone I've ever met, but cook? In a million years, I would never have guessed. Did you always want to cook?"

Trevor chuckled. "No. I think it was your mom who first planted the seed in my mind. She loved the process of cooking, and the food she prepared was delicious. When you left town, I missed those wonderful meals. As you might remember, my mom didn't cook. At all. Opening a can of soup or heating up a frozen pizza was her version of making dinner."

"So, you learned to cook to eat in the manner you'd grown accustomed?"

"Not right away, but I did get a job at Pirates Pizza the summer after you left. I found that while I made better tips waiting tables, I preferred being in the kitchen. I came up with some original pizzas— most are considered to be gourmet—and I found a lot of satisfaction from preparing a meal others enjoyed. When the owner told me he wanted to retire in a few years, he suggested if I wanted to buy the place, we could work out some owner financing. That really intrigued me." Trevor held up a spoon with a piece of prawn and the sauce it was cooking in and offered me a bite.

"Oh my God. That's fabulous. What did you put in it to make it so…" I didn't have a word to describe what I wanted to say.

"Saffron. And a few other things."

Trevor drained the pasta and put half on each plate. Then he spooned the scampi over it. He took the bread out of the oven and sliced it while I transferred everything onto the dining table that was next to a window looking out to the sea.

He topped off our wineglasses, used a remote to turn on music and the gas fireplace, and held out my chair for me.

I sat down, closed my eyes, and mentally cursed. Damn if I wasn't being swept off my feet by this whole performance, and damn if being swept off my feet was the last thing I wanted to be.

"So, it seems as if I missed quite a lot while I was gone," I said in an attempt to quell the sexual tension that had suddenly permeated the room. "Tell me everything."

"Not a lot to tell," Trevor said as I took my first full bite of the delicious meal and let out an audible sigh. "The year after you left, the high school football team won the state title. I was offered not one but two scholarships to top-ranked universities. I loved playing football, but I turned them down."

"Why?" I asked after taking a sip of my wine.

"I thought about going to college. You were gone, and Mac was headed to MIT. I didn't really have a reason to stay, but I didn't feel like a four-year situation was right for me. I decided to take the offer to buy Pirates Pizza. It felt like a good fit."

"You seem happy."

"I am. I love owning the restaurant, and I love my life. And I love it a lot more now that you're back. I really did miss you."

I met Trevor's eyes with my own. "I missed you too. And I'm very happy to be back. It feels right to have you and Mac back in my life, and I'm excited about the concept of starting my own business. I've never worked for myself before. You'll have to give me some tips."

"The main thing is to be organized and stay on top of the bookkeeping. The first year I owned Pirates Pizza, I was a lot more relaxed about the bookkeeping than I should have been. Come tax time, I had a real mess on my hands. Luckily, I had some money put away to pay the fines I ended up owing, but I could have been in real trouble."

"I'm sure you'll be able to teach me a lot. It'll be nice to have a veteran business owner to help me get started. I had a friend who opened a boutique, and all the paperwork required to get the licensing she needed was crazy. Of course, I'll be working out of the house and won't have employees, so it should be easier."

"We'll sit down and come up with a plan," Trevor promised.

I put my hand over his. "Thanks. For everything. Really. I just got back here, and I already don't know what I'd do without you."

Trevor squeezed my hand, then pulled away. There was a look on his face I couldn't quite define. Not a negative look exactly. Just a look. Contemplative, I guess. I felt like I should say something but suddenly felt awkward, so I took a bite of my food and let the moment ride.

"So, you said you had news about Naomi Collins?" Trevor eventually said, breaking the silence and taking the conversation in another direction.

"I do. Not a lot, but I talked to Woody this morning. Based on a necklace found around the skeleton's neck, he's fairly certain we found Naomi Collins, and that she most likely died of blunt force trauma to the head, although there's evidence of a broken rib he didn't think was connected to her death.

Woody should know more when he gets the full report."

"Poor girl. Any conclusions about who might have killed her?"

I shook my head. "Not really, but we made a list. We started on a whiteboard, but I wrote everything down on a piece of paper. We can go over it after we eat, if you want. I think we ended up with ten possible suspects, including the ones you and I have already discussed. I think it's going to be tough to narrow things down after so much time unless I can connect to Naomi and she can tell us who killed her. For one thing, many of the suspects have left Cutter's Cove, so we can't even interview them."

"Maybe Woody can track them down," Trevor suggested.

"Yeah. He might be able to. My plan now has many fronts. First, I'm going to attempt to connect with Naomi. I really believe her telling me what happened is our best bet. And I'm going to try to talk to the people on the list who are still in the area. If one of them is guilty, he probably isn't going to talk, but I can talk to people who know them as well. Obviously, I'll be working with Woody; he has the best chance of getting anyone who might know what happened to talk. And finally, when Mac gets here, I'm going to have her do a thorough search into the backgrounds of each of the suspects. Even if we can't identify the killer, we might be able to pare down the list."

Trevor popped a plump prawn into his mouth. "It sounds as if you've given this some thought."

"I have. I had a lot of time to think, driving back and forth to Portland today."

"You know I'll help where I can," Trevor assured me.

"I know. And I value that quite a lot."

"What about Alyson? Is she still around?"

"I think she's gone. According to Chan, we'd be reintegrated as soon as I allowed her in and committed to staying here. I think that's happened. I haven't seen her around all day."

Trevor tilted his head so he could look closely at me. "How does that make you feel?"

"Surprisingly sad, yet I can feel her energy inside me, and that's nice." I remembered what a crush Alyson had on him and suddenly wondered if the attraction I was feeling now was coming from her rather than me. Of course, if we were united, perhaps that meant our feelings were the same. Geez, this was confusing. "I'd love to see the rest of this place," I said after a brief lull in the conversation.

"There isn't a lot of it, but I can provide the complete tour. Basically, I have the kitchen, dining, and living area down here, along with a half bath. Upstairs, there's the master bedroom, an office, and a full bath. It's not big, but it's enough for me. And the best part is, I can walk outside and go surfing whenever I want."

I set down my fork. "I've been here for three weeks. Why is it this is the first time you've brought me here? We even went surfing that day. We could just as easily have come here."

"Honestly?"

I nodded.

"I didn't want to bring you too firmly into my life. You showed up after ten years, and while I was happy to see you, I knew you'd be leaving. The last time you left, it almost destroyed me. Mac too. We were like a family. We loved you. And then, in the blink of an eye, you were gone."

I huffed out a breath. I didn't think it was possible for me to feel any worse about how I'd handled things, but suddenly I did.

"I'm not saying this to make you feel bad," Trevor continued. "I just wanted you to understand why I didn't open the door too wide before you decided to stay. Until you broke up with Ethan. Until I believed I could open up to you without getting hurt."

"I'm sorry," I said, and meant it more than mere words could convey. "I handled things badly before, but I'm not the same person I was ten years ago. I know what I want now, and I no longer feel I have two worlds competing for my attention. I've chosen this one. I'm here to stay."

Trevor tossed his napkin on the table, stood up, and grabbed my hand. "Come on. I'll show you the upstairs and then the best part."

"Best part?" I lifted a brow.

"The garage."

"The garage is the best part of the house? I know you always had a thing for cars, but I doubt any garage can top this totally awesome house."

Trevor pulled me to my feet. "Just wait. You'll see."

And Trevor was right. Not only was the upstairs as wonderful as the downstairs, but the double-car garage not only housed Raquel, the 1965 Ford Mustang he'd inherited from his grandfather, but a work area where he made furniture and other items out of the driftwood he found on the beach.

"Wow," I said as I picked up a large piece of wood he was forming into a bowl. "I love this." I looked up and smiled. "It seems, Trevor Johnson, you're a man of many talents."

"My work isn't gallery quality. Yet. But I've sold a few pieces in shops in the area, and second to cooking, woodworking helps me relax. I'd love to make you something for the house now that you're staying."

"That would be great."

"We'll go together to find a piece of wood that speaks to you. Maybe in the morning, after the storm blows through."

"Is the piece of wood really that important?"

"It's the soul that brings the art to life."

Chapter 7

Thursday, June 14

It had poured all day yesterday, so I'd stayed home and begun making plans for my future. A future, I told myself, that included Trevor as a friend and only a friend. I wasn't certain what sort of insanity had gripped me on Tuesday night, having me thinking thoughts of romance. Trevor and I were friends long ago, and I'd been around the block enough times to know that mixing desire and friendship was never a good idea.

After a bit of introspection, I'd decided it was most definitely the newly integrated Alyson, with her teenage hormones, that had me thinking of gentle kisses, lingering touches, and nights of passion with Trev I would surely regret. No, a romantic interlude with him was just one of those things I'd keep locked away in my thoughts. In my dreams. In my imagination.

Changing my train of thought this morning, I rolled out of bed and slipped a sweatshirt over my head against the morning chill. As I walked downstairs to make coffee, I forced my mind to Naomi. I'd wanted to go back to visit with her yesterday, but with all the rain, that seemed impractical. Getting pneumonia wasn't going to help me help her, so I'd stayed in and spent way too much time in my head. Today, I vowed, was going to be a day of action. I'd urge Naomi to make an appearance and convince her to trust me. This was the day I'd take a giant step forward in finding her killer and setting both her and myself free from whatever unfinished business bound her to this world and me.

I sipped my coffee and watched the sky change from black to gray to pink and then to orange, with a tinge of purple to make the sunrise truly exceptional. Naomi had come to me in my dreams the past two nights. I hadn't been able to speak to her directly, to ask questions and receive answers, but I'd seen her and felt her presence. I didn't know if she would remember what had happened to her even if I was able to make a direct connection. Booker hadn't remembered his death, at least not at first. But with time, the things he'd blocked from his mind had begun to reemerge, and eventually, I'd been able to find out who had killed him and then release him from the earthly plane.

Shadow jumped into my lap and began to purr. I scratched him beneath the chin as he circled and settled. Sunny was chewing on a rawhide and Tucker was sleeping peacefully at my side. I set my mug on the cheery blue table and settled in to watch the sun rise from beyond the hill to the east. I was surprised Mom hadn't joined me this morning, though the fervor that gripped her when she felt inspired to paint had kept her up late for several nights in a row. One thing was certain: her time in Cutter's Cove was providing a lot of new work to display in her gallery when she returned to New York.

The sun had just shown the top of its shiny head when my phone dinged, indicating I had a text. It was from Trevor, letting me know he had lattes and pastries if I was awake. I texted back that I was on the deck and to come on around.

I looked down at the old sweatshirt I'd pulled on, the boy's shorts I'd worn to sleep, and the bare feet resting on the railing in front of me. My hair was tousled and my face bare of makeup. Heck, I hadn't even brushed my teeth. I should go in and wash up before he arrived, but I popped a stick of gum in my mouth and forced myself to stay put. *Just a friend*, I reminded myself. If it was Mac on her way over, I wouldn't give worn-out shorts and a tattered sweatshirt a second thought. *Just a friend*, I repeated. If bed hair and sleep-filled eyes were good enough for Mac, they were good enough for Trevor.

"Oh crap," I said aloud as I heard his truck on the road leading to the house. I pushed Shadow off my lap, leaped to my feet, and ran into the house. There were clean clothes in the laundry room off the kitchen, and I washed my face and rinsed out my mouth in the half bath, finger-combed my hair, slipped into jeans and a clean sweatshirt over the tank I'd worn to bed, then hurried back out to the deck, where Trevor was just rounding the corner from the drive.

"What a beautiful morning after all that rain," Trevor said as he sat down on a chair next to me. He handed me a tall latte from a nearby coffee bar.

"Nonfat?"

"Of course," he answered. "Which seems somewhat ridiculous because the pastries you prefer have at least twice the calories as almost any other pastry the place sells."

I shrugged as I accepted the paper bag Trevor handed me. "If I don't have a high-calorie drink I can have a high-calorie treat." I took the flaky pastry out of the bag and took a bite. Absolute heaven.

"I talked to Mac last night," Trevor offered. "She said she's leaving early and should be here by late afternoon. I'm going to let my manager handle things and take the day off. The three of us have some catching up to do."

I licked the sugar from my lips. "We will. I know she's only been gone for a little over a week, but what a week it's been. I'm excited to see her. Did she say exactly what time she'll be here?"

"Not exactly, but I guess around four. Do you have plans today?"

"I wanted to go back to the gravesite to try to connect with Naomi. I also thought I'd have a chat with Woody. I'm hoping he's made some progress narrowing down the list of suspects, because so far, I haven't. I'm thinking of buying a whiteboard and setting up a murder board here like the one he has at the station."

"That's a good idea. I can come with you to visit Naomi, buy the board, and meet with Woody if you want."

I crossed my legs and tucked them beneath me. "Fine with me if you have the time. I'm going to take the dogs for a long walk before I go. You can come along if you'd like."

"I'd like that very much."

I left Trevor with Shadow and the dogs while I went in, changed my clothes once again, and gave my face a good wash and my teeth a real brush. I put a clip in my hair, pulled some old Nike's onto my bare feet, and then headed back to the stairs. Mom was coming out of her bedroom as I passed, so I told her that Trevor was here and what we planned to do for the day. She was going to grab a bite to eat, then head up to her studio, as usual. I reminded her that Mac was arriving later today, and she offered to make something for dinner. I promised to text her later to let her know what our plans were going to be.

"I'm all set," I said as I wandered back onto the deck.

Trevor set aside Shadow, who had been sitting happily in his lap, then stood up. I motioned for the dogs to follow, then started down to the drive. After circling the house, we headed down the trail that hugged the drop to the sea. I'd walked along this trail hundreds of times, but the view still had the ability to awe and amaze me. The brilliance of the sky. The deep blue of the sea. Gray rocks, jagged and sharp. Rolling hills carpeted in varying shades of green. This bluff, this little piece of shoreline, belonged to me, and I wouldn't have it any other way.

"I spent some time going through the house yesterday," I said, mostly to break the silence. "I love what Mom did with it ten years ago, but I want to make a few changes. Nothing drastic, just a few things to make the space mine."

"Makes sense. Are you thinking of buying the house from your mother?"

"She's giving it to me. She doesn't need the money she put into it, and it seemed easier this way. Her attorney is drawing up the paperwork. I'll take over the taxes, insurance, and maintenance."

"Seven bedrooms, nine fireplaces, three bathrooms, an attic, and a basement seems like a lot of house for one person," Trevor pointed out.

"Maybe. But it isn't just me. It's me and Shadow, Tucker, and Sunny, and of course Mac, because I plan to give her her own room as a means of enticing her to visit often. I also want Mom to keep her bedroom and space in the attic, which I thought we could share. Really, if you think about it, seven bedrooms is barely enough."

Trevor wound his fingers through mine the way he had dozens of times before. Just friends holding hands, I reminded myself, as my heartbeat rose just a bit. Nothing romantic, nothing proprietary. Just friends.

"I thought I'd start downstairs," I said as we settled into an easy pace.

"Please tell me you aren't going to touch the kitchen. It's perfect the way it is."

"No," I assured him. "Not the kitchen. I did think I'd buy some accessory items in dark gray to go with the white plates, cobalt blue bowls, and light blue glassware. Accents to add depth to the mix."

"I like the idea. Maybe some pieces to set out on the counter like a ceramic jug with light blue flowers or a bowl with fresh fruit."

"Exactly." I paused to make sure we weren't walking too fast for Tucker, then continued. "I want to change the rug in the main living area and maybe buy a new sofa for the parlor. The dining table is great, but I always thought it would be nice to find a hutch to anchor one end of the room."

"There's a great antique barn down the coast. Many of their pieces need refinishing, but luckily for you, you have a friend who's all set up to handle the repair and refurbishing."

I turned my head. "You'd do that?"

"Absolutely. I enjoy bringing new life to old pieces."

"So, you can cook and refinish furniture. What did you do with the Trevor Johnson who could barely heat soup and thought TV trays were superior to dining tables?"

Trevor shrugged. "He grew up." He stopped walking, and we stood looking out at the sea. "I guess we all did."

"I guess we did."

"Sometimes, when Mac and I get together, we talk about the silly things we used to do, say, and believe. And while those silly things are in the past, they're *our* past, and they matter."

I had to agree with that. Things of the past did matter. "I often think of that Christmas, when you took Mac and me on a sleigh ride. There was no snow that year, and the sleigh had wheels, but I remember the lights and the cozy feel of the blanket we wrapped around ourselves to hold back the chill in the air."

"That was the Christmas you almost fell to your death from the Ferris wheel at Hometown Christmas," Trevor reminded me.

"Another memory, for sure. Not quite as warm and friendly as the first, but still relevant. Whenever I think of you dressed as Santa and Mac and me as elves, I get a warm feeling inside. We were involved. We participated in the community. We made a difference."

Tucker slipped his head under my hand. "And we can't forget about Tucker the Red-Nosed Reindeer," I said with a laugh.

"Or the ridiculous costumes we wore in the community play," Trevor added.

"Or the little girl who sat on Santa's lap and asked him to bring her mommy home." I looked at Trevor and smiled. "Or the Santa who did."

Trev shrugged. "We all reunited that little girl with her mother, the way we all pitched in to make sure Hometown Christmas went off without a hitch and brought in a killer. We were, and are, a good team. You and me and Mac."

I leaned my head on Trevor's shoulder as we paused on the bluff and looked out toward the sea. "We really are."

Trevor wove his fingers through mine and gave them a slight squeeze, then took a step away. "We should head back if you want to drive out and try to connect with Naomi before we meet with Woody."

"Yeah, we should."

******

When we arrived at the bluff, Trevor went down to the beach with the dogs while I took the dirt trail to the grave. I had little expectation that Naomi would make an appearance, but the odds were greater if I was alone. As I had before, I took a seat on a rock, looked out to the sea, and began to speak.

"Are you here, Naomi? It's me. Amanda."

I waited as the sound of the waves lulled me into a state of semicontentment despite my frustration at my inability to connect with Naomi. Even though I didn't see or hear her, I could feel her lurking, so I proceeded as if she were listening. "Now that we've found your body, the police are looking into things. Unfortunately, we have a pretty long list of suspects. Unless we come across someone who knows what happened and is willing to talk, it might take us months to weed through them." I sat in silence for a moment before I continued. "I'm sure remembering is hard for you. I can't imagine how hard it must be. Someone you knew, possibly even cared for, ended your life, and that must be the worst kind of betrayal. Many people think it was your father who did it, the police included. I guess the idea has merit, considering his history."

Again I waited for a sign from Naomi that she was there and listening. When she didn't appear or speak, I began again. "Jeffrey Kline makes a good suspect as well. You were a child and he was a grown man. There was talk he traded his knowledge of music for your innocence."

No, I heard in my mind. I still couldn't see Naomi, but I could hear the echo of her voice. It sounded as if she was far away. As if she was speaking through a tunnel that echoed her thoughts rather than actually voicing them.

"No?" I asked. "No, he didn't trade music lessons for sex, or no, he didn't kill you?"

No, I heard again. This time the voice was clearer.

"I'm listening if you want to explain," I said. I hoped she'd appear, but somehow, I doubted she would. It was important to be patient, not to scare her off. She certainly was a skittish ghost, though who could blame her? She'd lived her whole life trying to stay in the shadows.

Eventually, I heard a voice. "Mr. Kline was my friend. He was nice to me. He taught me to play the piano. He wouldn't hurt me."

I closed my eyes and focused on the sound of Naomi's voice. I could hear a soft melody playing in the background. The haunting song could be an echo of her memory merging with my consciousness.

"So he didn't ask for sex?"

"He was my friend."

I noticed Naomi hadn't really answered my question, but I let it go. At least for now. "If Mr. Kline didn't hurt you, do you remember who did?"

"I have to go."

And the voice and melody were gone. I was disappointed I hadn't gotten more, but it was something. Naomi had shared her thoughts with me. Intentional thoughts, not just an echo from the past. That was progress in my book. I told Naomi I'd be back, then got up and went to look for Trevor.

"Any luck?" he asked as I joined him and the dogs on the beach.

I bent down to greet my canine companions, who were wiggling and wagging at my feet. "Some. Naomi didn't appear, but she spoke to me."

"Did she tell you who killed her?"

"No. But she defended Jeffrey Kline. She said he was her friend and taught her to play the piano. She said he would never hurt her."

"Do you believe her?"

I considered the question. "I don't know. Naomi sounded certain he wouldn't hurt her, but I think she evaded my question about her giving him sex in exchange for the music lessons. It's possible Mr. Kline did sleep with her but didn't kill her. Or maybe he was just a nice man who befriended a lonely child and really was innocent on all counts."

"What now?" Trevor asked.

"I guess I keep coming back, keep trying. Eventually, I think I'll find a way to get through to her. In the meantime, let's go see Woody."

We turned and headed back to the parking area. The warm breeze caressed and calmed me as we navigated the hilly path. "When I was talking with Naomi, there was soft music in the background. It felt like the memory of a song. Her memory."

"Do you think it's important?" Trevor asked.

"Maybe. It was a familiar song, but not a popular one. I think it must have been old. I felt as if I should have recognized it, but I couldn't grab hold of what it was."

Trevor put his arm around my shoulders as we continued to the parking area. "Give it time. It'll come to you."

******

I called ahead, and Woody was waiting for us in the conference room where we'd set up the whiteboard a few days before. He'd made some notes, drawn some lines, and crossed off two names since then. "It looks like you've been working," I said after we'd settled around the table.

"That's my job," Woody reminded me. "Besides, the murder of a sixteen-year-old with so much life ahead of her sticks in my craw."

"It really does," I seconded. "I see you have Jeffrey Kline's name highlighted."

Woody nodded. "I managed to track him down. He's married now, with two children. He said he was visiting his sister in Wisconsin when Naomi went missing. He remembered it specifically because it affected him deeply that she simply disappeared. Darwin Young spoke to Jane Smith back then. She was his colleague, and she's now his wife. She confirmed he was out of town during the days he said he was away."

"If she's his wife, she could be lying," I pointed out.

"That's true. I tried contacting the sister, but so far, she hasn't returned my calls. I also have a call in to the school district. If Kline took days off from work, there should be a record of it. It was a long time ago, but payroll records are something offices and businesses usually keep forever."

"It sounds like verifying whether he was in town should be doable." I frowned. "I'm curious about the wife, though. I remember hearing that Kline left town shortly after Naomi disappeared. How did a colleague at the time of the disappearance end up as his wife?"

"According to Jane Kline, the pair were dating casually beforehand. It sounded as if their relationship intensified after Naomi went missing. When he left town, she followed."

Okay, it could have happened that way. A nagging in the back of my mind said there was more to it than that, but I could accept the explanation for now. "If it wasn't for the fact that Naomi herself told me that Mr. Kline was her friend and hadn't hurt her, I'd suspect the authenticity of the alibi. Let's leave the music teacher on the list until we hear back from the sister and the school district."

"You made a connection with Naomi?" Woody asked.

"A very brief one. I didn't learn anything other than that Naomi seemed to have really liked Mr. Kline and was certain he wouldn't hurt her. I tried to push for more, but she faded away. I'll try again tomorrow. What else do you have?"

"I spoke in depth to Greg Dalton. In my opinion, he isn't the guy we're looking for. We don't know exactly when Naomi was killed, so it's hard to match alibis with it, but I think he was telling the truth when he admitted he'd asked Naomi out as a prank. He said he had ended up having a really good time with her. He had a girlfriend already and wasn't looking for anything from Naomi, but he doesn't seem to have wished her any harm. I've been a cop long enough that I can usually pick up when someone's lying. Dalton didn't seem to be."

"Okay," I said. "He was a long shot anyway. Did he tell you who was behind the prank in the first place?"

"He wouldn't say, just that someone at school gave him a wad of cash to ask Naomi out. He needed the money, so he did it."

"Seems odd," Trevor commented.

"Maybe. But kids can be cruel, and even nice ones like Naomi can make enemies. I suspect whoever paid Greg knew tongues would wag if she agreed to go out with him. Maybe that was enough to serve as a form of revenge."

Yeah okay. Maybe. "Anything else?"

"Toad was the high-school nickname of Zander Barrington."

"Zander Barrington the tech guy?" I asked.

"One and the same. I spoke to him about Naomi, and while he admitted to finding her aloofness interesting when he was a teen, and he did have a bit of a crush on her, he didn't know her all that well. His recollection of the timeline was a bit fuzzy, but he thought she left town a couple of weeks after they went to a movie with a larger group of kids from the chess club. He hadn't heard she'd been found dead and seemed genuinely shocked when I told him."

"I think Mac is friends with him," Trevor volunteered. "We can ask her about it when she gets here. Mac is a good judge of character. If he wasn't on the up and up, she'd know it."

"I think we can clear him," Woody said. "Although it might not hurt to mention him to Mac when you see her."

"So, that leaves Naomi's father, Bodine Collins; the transient, Frank Joplin; her classmate and all-around scum of a guy, Wade Stone; Ron Pullman, the man who was working next door and is now a registered sex offender; Carl Woodbine, the husband of the woman Bodine Collins was sleeping with; Peter Steadman, the creepy high school janitor; and the unnamed guy on the Harley."

"That about sums it up," Woody confirmed. "I've got some feelers out, so hopefully I'll have more information to add to the mix by tomorrow."

"Okay, thanks." I stood up. "I'm going to try to connect with Naomi again too. And when Mac gets here, she should be able to dig a bit deeper online. I feel confident we'll get to the bottom of this sooner rather than later."

Woody looked doubtful. "Really?"

I tilted my head. "Okay, maybe not sooner," I admitted. "But I'm committed to keep plugging away at it as long as it takes."

We left the police station, and planned to go back to my house. Mac would arrive today, and I didn't want to miss her. I knew she'd be as happy as I was that I was staying, so a celebratory dinner would be just the thing. Trevor had offered to cook, so I'd texted Mom to let her know, and we stopped by the grocery store for the things Trev would need to work his magic.

Chapter 8

When I heard a car in the drive, I was expecting to see Mac's little VW Bug. I don't know why I assumed she'd have kept the same car she'd inherited from her grandmother when she was in high school. That was ten years ago, after all.

"You have an SUV," I said as Mac pulled to a stop. "It's gorgeous. And full," I said when I noticed the vehicle looked to be packed with everything she owned.

"I told you I was driving so I could bring my equipment."

"You did. But I guess I thought *equipment* would run to a computer, and maybe a printer."

Mac opened the door and got out. I hugged her and then moved back so Trevor could do the same.

"Don't worry," Mac said. "I'm not going to haul all this into your house. I just wanted to bring what I'd need to get started when I find an apartment."

"You're staying?" I screeched.

"I'm staying," Mac confirmed.

"For good?" Trevor asked.

Mac nodded.

"Hot damn." Trevor picked her up and twirled her around, the way he had me.

"Put me down before you make me puke." Mac laughed as she clung to his shoulders.

Trevor swung her around a few more times, then complied. "I can't believe it. What about your job?"

"I quit."

Trevor raised a brow. "Just like that?"

"Just like that. I haven't been happy there for a while. What I really want to do is start my own software firm. Being back and spending time with both of you a couple of weeks ago convinced me now was the time. I have a lot to do to get something off the ground, but I have clients who are willing to make the jump with me, and I have a good reputation to work from. I can do what I do from anywhere." Mac looked at me. "I hoped you'd let me stay with you until I can find an apartment. I'll start looking tomorrow."

I wrapped her in my arms. "No need to look; you can stay here. With me. In the house."

Mac looked uncertain. "You mean until you go back?"

I shook my head. "I'm not going back. Well, maybe until I can pack my stuff and sell my apartment. I'm taking over the house from Mom. I'm staying."

"Staying?"

I nodded. "It seems we're both starting new ventures."

Trevor put an arm around each of us. "You have no idea how happy I am to have both my girls back in Cutter's Cove."

Just then, Mom came out, and the hugging and celebrating began anew. Once we were all hugged out, Trevor and I began helping Mac unpack. After a bit of discussion, we started setting her up on the third floor. No one was using it, and there were three rooms and a bath, so she could use one of them as a bedroom, one as an office, and one as a guest room should any of her siblings come for a visit. Mom and I had bedrooms on the second floor. We shared a bath, but I was thinking about taking out a wall between my bedroom and the guest room to create a master suite.

I helped Mac unpack her clothes and make up her bed while Trevor was downstairs starting dinner. The evening was warm and beautiful, so we decided to set the outdoor table and eat our meal, which I was sure was going to be exceptional, overlooking the sea.

"Did you know Trev could cook?" I asked her, as I helped to hang clothes in her closet.

"Sure. He took classes and everything. He can even bake. You seriously haven't lived until you've had his tiramisu."

I paused with a hanger in my hand. "I had no idea, which isn't surprising because I didn't keep in touch. But that's changing now. We're back. All of us together in one town."

Mac grinned. "I still can't believe you're staying. Why didn't you tell me?"

"I just decided two days ago, and I wanted it to be a surprise. I guess in retrospect I should have called you. It would have been tragic if you'd already rented an apartment. Of course, I had no idea you planned to stay in town, so I had no reason to think time was of the essence. When exactly did you make your decision?"

"I think the seed was planted when I was here. You asked about my job, and I realized how incredibly bored I was with it. I'd been mulling over the idea of starting my own firm, but I was waiting for the right time. Somehow, it suddenly felt right, I put my plan into action when I got back to California. Your staying is a bonus I wasn't expecting." Mac looked around the room. "And free rent will help. At least at first."

"Stay as long as you want. I wasn't as thrilled about living alone once Mom went back to New York as I let on."

"You have Alyson," Mac pointed out.

I sat down on the side of Mac's bed. "Not really. Not the way I did. It seems now that I've decided to stay, we've merged into a unified whole. I haven't seen her in days."

Mac sat down next to me. "You'd think reintegration would be a good thing, but your tone of voice indicates otherwise."

"It's confusing," I admitted. "I'm glad I'm no longer fragmented. I feel happier than I have in a very long time. And Alyson's youthful energy is mine, which is nice. But I guess I'd gotten used to having her to talk to and hang out with." I took Mac's hand in mine. "But now I have you."

Mac hugged me.

"Let's see what Trev is cooking up," I said. "We can finish your unpacking later."

"I am hungry. Maybe we can snag a preview," Mac suggested.

"If not, I have cheese and crackers. Though I'd hate to spoil my appetite. He made me scampi the other night, which was the best thing I'd ever eaten, and I've eaten in a lot of five-star restaurants."

"When Trev told me he was going to take cooking classes, I was surprised. He does like to eat, so I guess it isn't that much of a stretch. I think the owner of Pirates Pizza offering to sell to him was what clinched the deal."

"I missed so much," I said as I headed down the stairs. "I need to catch up on everything. I thought maybe…" I stopped talking halfway down the stairs. "The lasagna smells wonderful."

"Trev uses five kinds of cheese in his lasagna," Mac informed me. "It really is to die for. Of all the food he's made for me over the years, his lasagna is my favorite."

"That's what he said when we stopped at the market to buy the ingredients. I can't wait to taste it. Mom's lasagna is pretty spectacular, but this smells amazing."

"Do you still like to cook?" Mac asked as we began moving again.

I ran a hand over the smooth railing as we descended the stairs. "I like to cook, and plan to do more of it now that I'm back in Cutter's Cove. I didn't really have the time in New York. Ethan and I usually ate out, or if he wasn't around, I'd just pop something into the microwave."

"Speaking of Ethan," Mac said as we reached the landing on the first floor, "what does he think about your move?"

"When I called to break up with him, he almost seemed relieved. Things have been over for quite some time; we were just too busy to notice."

When we walked into the kitchen we found Trevor chopping vegetables for a salad, while Mom sat at the bar talking to him. Now that was a flip from the norm.

"It smells delicious in here," I said.

"One of the reasons I love Italian food is because it smells so good while it's cooking," Trevor answered. "Your mom and I were just about to take a bottle of wine onto the deck while the lasagna bakes. Would the two of you like a glass?"

The evening was warm, the air calm. Large waves rolled gently onto the beach, breaking at the last minute, almost like an afterthought. Seagulls circled overhead, scouting for the unlucky fish that would be their dinner. The sun had begun its descent toward the horizon as boats with white sails drifted slowly out toward the open sea to watch it set. If sunrises in this house were spectacular, sunsets were indescribably breathtaking. I sat down between Mom and Trevor, who sat between Mac and me.

"What a great way to end the day." Mac sighed in contentment.

"It's the best," I agreed as Sunny lumbered over and put her head in my lap. I reached down to pet her, hoping Tucker wouldn't be jealous. He seemed fine having a second dog in the house, but then, he'd always been easygoing. I wondered if Mom would miss having him with her. Tucker was too old to travel back and forth across the country, but perhaps a small dog that would fit in an airline-approved carrier and could be trained for travel would be just the thing. I'd have to talk to her about it before she left.

"So, tell me about the new mystery you're working on," Mac said after a while. "Trev filled me in on the basics, but I want to help."

We took turns telling Mac what we knew. She interrupted to ask questions, and it didn't take long for her to get up to speed.

"Do you think Naomi knows who killed her?" Mac asked.

"I don't know. She's skittish. She has yet to materialize, and I can only get very brief comments from her when she speaks at all. In my opinion, the person who killed her cared about her, so while we're researching people like the man working on the neighbor's house and the high school janitor, I don't think either of them will turn out to be the killer."

"Why do you think she was killed by someone who cares about her?" Mac asked.

"Because of the grave. It seemed care was taken to choose a beautiful, peaceful setting. It was tucked away where it wasn't likely to be found, yet it was close to the sea on a beautiful knoll, marked with a handmade cross. Some random killer probably wouldn't have gone to so much trouble. There are a lot of places it would have been easier to dump a body if you just didn't want it to be found."

"Makes sense." Mac nodded.

"It's all so tragic," Mom added. "To have you life taken from you before you've even had a chan to live has to be its own kind of hell, but to hav taken by someone you knew and possibly even (about."

"It has to feel like the ultimate betrayal," I finished.

"Do you suspect the father?" Mac asked.

I frowned. Did I? "I'm not sure. Maybe. Though something about the father as the killer doesn't ring true to me. Based on what I've learned, he was a violent man who drank too much, and it does seem as if he might have been the last person to see her alive, but I don't know." I tried to sort out my thoughts, which had become jumbled over the course of the past couple of days.

"If you're going with the theory that the killer was someone who cared about Naomi, who else could it be but the father?" Mac asked.

"Jeffrey Kline, the music teacher, or someone else in Naomi's life we haven't yet identified." I took in a frustrated breath. "I need to get Naomi to talk to me. Getting her to share her memories, even if they're fragmented, is the best chance of figuring out what happened to her."

Mom placed her hand on my arm. "Give it time. You're good at this. You'll figure it out."

I squeezed Mom's hand. "Thanks, Mom. Sometimes I need some encouragement."

Trevor stood up with his empty wineglass. "The lasagna should be about done. I'll put the bread in the oven."

"I'll set the table," Mac offered, rising as well.

Mom offered to help, and I grabbed my camera to capture the last whisper of daylight as the sky, streaked with orange and red, slowly faded to gray. One of my favorite times of day was the brief breath between light and darkness, when colors faded and the trees on the hillside slowly disappeared from sight. The silhouette of ordinary objects took on a mysterious sensation in those few minutes before the sky darkened completely and stars began to litter the sky. My work with my camera had shown me that beauty could be found in commonplace objects if they were captured in the right light or at the right angle. A tree limb that had washed up onto the beach could add texture to the otherwise flat surface of the sand and the sea.

I kept snapping shots, changing position, angling the camera, trying different lenses. When the sky was completely dark, I stopped and looked toward the horizon.

"Anything interesting?" Mom asked.

I held up the viewing window of the camera and began to flip though the shots I'd taken. "I especially like this one." I paused at the image of the sky turning dark, yet still light enough so the silhouettes of seagulls in flight over the rocky shore was clearly visible. "I think I might play with the tones a bit. If it turns out the way I hope, I'll print and matte it. The gray is exactly the color I want to bring into the house."

"I love this one with all the purple," Mom said. "Print it for me? I think this might just be the subject of a new painting."

"You're going to need a truck to get all the paintings you've been working on here to New York."

Mom shrugged. "If I need a truck I can rent one, but airplanes have plenty of room in cargo. It looks like the food is on the table."

I hooked my arm through hers and we joined Mac and Trevor. This, I thought, was the way I wanted t end every day. With everyone I loved in the world sitting around the table sharing a meal and talking about our day.

Chapter 9

Saturday, June 16

The dream had returned, more vivid, more intense, than before. I supposed its sheer energy could be the result of the time I'd spent on the little knoll, trying to bond with Naomi, the previous day. Mac had been setting up her office, Trevor was at work, and Mom was sequestered in the attic painting, so I'd taken the time I thought I'd need to finally connect with the young girl.

For a long time I'd sat alone, looking out at the sea. I waited patiently for her to come to me. I hoped she would trust me enough to seek me out. I was alone for quite some time, but at last I began to hear the music. It was the same melody I'd heard before. A tune I was certain was familiar to me, yet not identifiable to my conscious mind. The seductive song was being played on a piano that was so far away it seemed more like an echo. Or maybe a memory. The haunting song spoke of loss. Despair. Longing.

Before coming to the bluff, I'd spent an hour with Woody going over the suspect list again. He'd gotten alibis for, and managed to definitively eliminate, Greg Dalton, Zander Barrington, Wade Stone, Peter Steadman, and Ron Pullman. That left Naomi's father, Bodine Collins; Carl Woodbine, the husband of the woman Collins was having an affair with; Frank Joplin, the homeless man Naomi was seen talking to; and the guy on the Harley. Due mostly to my gut feeling that Jeffrey Kline fit the profile for the killer, he was still on the list. Woody had pulled his employment record with the school board. He'd taken time off at the beginning of the week Naomi went missing, which matched his assertion that he'd been visiting his sister, but he was back in town by midweek, and because we didn't know for certain when Naomi had died, it was possible he was the killer.

I sat up and looked around my still-dark room. It was early, but the dream had shattered any hope I had of sleep. I got up and pulled on some warm sweatpants and a matching sweatshirt. Slipping my Nike's onto my feet, I grabbed a flashlight and went downstairs. Mac and Mom probably wouldn't be up for hours, but that was fine. I needed quiet time to think. Opening the front door, I stepped out into the cool morning air. Tucker and Sunny followed closely behind me, and I made my way to the bluff trail. The waves crashed in the distance, and a light breeze coming from the west caressed my face as I lifted it to the inky dark sky. It was peaceful out here on the bluff, where my only company other than the dogs were the twinkling stars overhead. I closed my eyes as the power of the sea steeped into my soul, as it had a hundred times before.

"What are you trying to tell me?" I whispered as the dream came to the forefront of my mind. It had started, as it always did, with me walking over the rolling hills that led to the isolated gravesite. In the past, I'd stood passively as I let images wash through my mind. But this time, I'd fallen to my knees, terror engulfing me. I began to sink to the ground, as if joining Naomi there in the dark, in the hell where she'd been waiting all these years.

I opened my eyes as my heart began to race again. The dream had felt so real. I could still feel the panic I had as the earth swallowed me one breath at a time. As far as I knew, Naomi hadn't been buried alive. At least I hoped not. Woody said she'd suffered a head injury that was assumed to have been fatal.

I wondered if Naomi somehow was the source of the dreams. If, for some reason, she came to me in the dead of night when the world was quiet and my mind relaxed. She hadn't yet appeared in ghostly form at any time, but during the night, when there was no one to see... Was she afraid? Ashamed? Had whatever had happened to her been so traumatic that even in death she felt the need to hide? I supposed the only one who had the answers to these questions was Naomi herself, so I'd wait, and listen, and try to understand the message I somehow knew would someday be mine to determine.

Tucker and Sunny sat at my feet, perhaps wondering why we were standing around out here in the dark when a perfectly good house with light, and warmth, and breakfast awaited. I sent a silent plea to Naomi, then turned around and walked back along the path with only my flashlight to guide me. Today would be another day. I'd try again. I'd try every day until I made the connection I needed. I supposed I could be wasting my time. If Naomi wanted my help, wouldn't she accept what I offered? But I didn't think a lack of desire on her part was what was going on. It was something else, something shocking that kept Naomi cowering in the dark.

Mac joined me on the deck just as the sky began to turn to gold. The sun hadn't yet peeked over the horizon, but its promise was already evident in the changing colors, now gold, then pink, then red.

"Do you need a refill on your coffee?" she asked.

"No. Thank you. I've had four cups already. I should probably quit before I end up spending the whole day bouncing off the walls."

Mac slid into the chair next to me as red turned to blue. "Four cups. You must have gotten up early."

"Couldn't sleep."

"The dream you told me about?"

I yawned and nodded.

"Maybe you should take today off. Recharge a bit after the long day you put in yesterday."

I reached my arms over my head in a gentle stretch. "No. I need to finish this. I realize that in many ways I'm no closer to solving this mystery than I was when I started, yet I know I'm close. I can feel it. The answer. Just out of my reach but oh so close."

"Sounds frustrating."

"Very frustrating." I turned slightly in my chair. "Are you planning to work today?"

"For a while. I got everything set up yesterday. I want to contact the clients I hope will follow me to let them know what I'm doing. I'm not quite ready to open my doors, but I want to provide a timeline so anyone who's wondering what became of me will know."

"Trev invited us over to his place tonight. He won't close until nine tonight, so he wasn't thinking dinner. He mentioned wine, and it's supposed to be warm this evening. Maybe sitting out on his deck and watching the waves roll in?"

"Sounds nice," Mac agreed. "He does have an awesome spot right on the sand."

"It's absolutely gorgeous. I'll admit I was shocked when he brought me home to dinner. I was expecting pizza, either in the restaurant or in a tiny apartment somewhere. When I saw his house on the beach and he cooked me scampi, I was speechless. Absolutely speechless."

"Trev has worked hard. He's done well for himself," Mac said. "I always knew he'd do something spectacular with his life."

I scrunched up my nose. "Really? I kind of thought of him as a slacker in high school."

Mac raised a brow. "A slacker? He was a star football, basketball, and baseball player, who worked hard, practiced religiously, and helped take all three teams to the state championships. He had a part-time job he used to maintain his car and pay his own expenses, and he had a decent grade point average while taking some of the same advance placement classes we did."

I narrowed my gaze. "I guess you're right. I don't know where the slacker impression came from.

Maybe he just made things look easy. Like he wasn't really trying. Wow," I said as the reality of what Mac had said sank in. "How could I have been so wrong?"

Mac shrugged. "I get it. You had your own stuff going on, and Trev was a bit of a goofball. I'm sure you weren't the only one who didn't realize how exceptional the guy beneath the superhero T-shirts, silly jokes, and casual approach to life really was."

"Maybe, but I'm not *most people*. Trev is and was one of my two best friends. He helped me solve all those mysteries. Sure, he wasn't as smart as you, but no one is. I should have noticed what you apparently did."

Mac didn't say anything, but I didn't expect her to. Mac and Trev had been friends since preschool. Given their easy way with each other, I'd wondered when I'd first met them if they were more than friends. Now, considering the way she'd leaped to his defense, I wondered the same thing again. Reason number four, I told myself, we were just friends. The last thing I wanted to do was make things awkward among us, and I didn't want to risk what the three of us had. I was more concerned than ever to bury any feelings of attraction I might be experiencing, especially now that I understood what an amazing man my goofy friend had grown up to be.

"I was thinking of making an omelet for breakfast. Mushroom and sausage. Are you interested?" I asked.

"Sounds great," Mac answered. "Do you need help?"

"No. Just relax. Enjoy the dawn of the new day. I'll bring the food out when it's ready."

"Are you planning on cooking for me every morning?" Mac asked with a grin on her face.

"Fat chance. I usually have yogurt or cereal for breakfast. Today, however, I find I'm in need of something with substance."

Mac leaned back in her chair and looked out to the sea, and I went into the house. Mom had worked late again last night, so I doubted we'd see her much before lunch. She'd always been something of a night owl, while I was an early riser. Maybe not quite as early as I'd woken this morning, though, I thought as I took eggs, sausage, mushrooms, and cheese from the refrigerator. But early; before the sun rose. In New York, I preferred to jog in the early hours, before most people were out of bed. I liked the quiet. The solitude. The opportunity to greet each new day as it dawned.

Grabbing some fresh herbs from the crisper, I sprinkled them over the eggs. Popping two pieces of bread in the toaster, I grabbed a pitcher of orange juice and two glasses and took them out to the deck. "Eggs will be ready in a minute if you need a coffee refill."

"Thanks, but I'll switch to juice," Mac said.

"Butter on your toast?"

"Always."

Mac was as skinny as she'd ever been. Skinnier, in fact. Yet she still seemed to eat like a linebacker most of the time. I supposed it took energy to do all the mental stuff she did every day. I'd maintained my high school weight as well, but I had to work at it. Mac didn't seem to need to. She never had. Good metabolism, I guess.

I transferred the omelets to plates and added the toast, grabbed the salt and pepper, and brought everything outside. The sun was rising by this point, glistening on the sea. I always enjoyed the promise of a new day, and today, I vowed, would be the one when I somehow managed to convince Naomi to trust me.

******

As I usually did, before I went to the gravesite, I stopped to check in with Woody. If he had news, I wanted to hear it. He'd been working hard to narrow down the suspects and focus on the details of Naomi's murder. The little nick on her rib, it turned out, was most likely the result of a break inflicted at some time earlier than the head injury that had killed her. What sort of hell had the poor girl been forced to endure? No wonder she was still skittish years after her death.

"I was hoping you'd stop by," Woody said as I entered his office.

"Do you have news?" I asked. My part in the investigation was to connect with Naomi, while Woody's was the usual police procedure, and so far, he'd been doing a lot better job than I had.

"While Jeffrey Kline indeed took off the Monday and Tuesday of the week Naomi went missing, he wasn't visiting his sister, as he claimed."

"Why would he lie about where he was?" I asked.

"The only explanation I can come up with is that he was doing something he didn't want anyone to know about."

"Like killing and burying Naomi."

Woody leaned forward, placing his elbows on the desk. "Perhaps. I have a call in to Kline and his wife, but I haven't heard from either of them yet. If I don't hear from Kline, I'll get in touch with the police in his town and have him brought in for questioning."

"So, the sister admitted he wasn't with her when he claimed he was?"

Woody shook his head. "No. The sister verified his alibi, but I dug around some more and found out she was on a business trip to Chicago during the time Kline said he was visiting her. I tracked down her ex-roommate, who told me he hadn't been there the entire time they'd lived together. It seems the brother and sister had a falling out, which, given the fact that she was willing to lie for him, they must have worked out."

I sat back in my chair and straightened my legs. "So, Jeffrey Kline is sounding guiltier by the hour."

"My money is on him or Bodine Collins. I haven't been able to track down the mysterious man on the Harley, or even confirm he ever existed. It made sense that if Naomi simply disappeared, some random guy might have given her a ride out of town. But now that we know she was killed and buried on the bluff, it looks more as if the killer must be someone she knew."

"I agree. I think we can take the guy on the Harley and the homeless man off the suspect list. What about Carl Woodbine, the husband of the woman Collins was having an affair with at the time of Naomi's death?"

"I've spoken to him several times. He divorced his wife and no longer shows evidence of rage over the affair, but it's been sixteen years, so the fact that he's over it isn't surprising. I didn't pick up a killer vibe when we spoke. He said his ex was a whore and Collins was a narcissist, and they both deserved what they got."

"Maybe you should see if you can find out where Kline actually was on the days he took off work. I'm going to pay Naomi another visit. Maybe she'll finally talk to me today."

"Do you really think she knows who killed her?" Woody asked.

I lifted a shoulder. "Maybe."

From the police station I went to the bluff where Naomi had been buried once again. The trip down the coast had become almost a daily ritual. I felt as if I was making progress with Naomi, even though it was slow. If I believed persistence could pay off, I needed to give Naomi the time to find the answers I sought.

I'd decided to bring Tucker with me today. Sunny was too young and energetic to be able to sit quietly for hours on end, but Tucker was old and tired enough to nap happily for as long as I needed him to. And it was possible Naomi might have liked dogs and decide to trust me if I showed up with one. The idea wasn't flawless, but anything was worth a shot at this point. Mac had agreed to keep an eye on Sunny, so Tucker and I settled down for our wait. Fortunately, it wasn't as long as I'd anticipated.

"Naomi," I said as I began to hear the music I associated with her.

Now, for the first time, Naomi appeared. Her image was faint, more of a shimmery shadow, but I could clearly make out the braid down her back, the casual shorts, the stick-thin frame. I could sense her uncertainty, so I moved slowly. Tucker had never sensed ghosts before, and Naomi was no different. He slept contentedly in the shade of a nearby tree, but I noticed Naomi glancing at him. It might have been a better choice to bring Shadow, who had seen and even interacted with ghosts in the past. Perhaps next time. If there needed to be a next time.

"The sea is so peaceful and calming, don't you think?" I asked.

"Beneath the peaceful surface you'll find death and darkness," Naomi said in a soft voice.

That was grim. I continued to sit perfectly still, so I wouldn't frighten her. "Perhaps. I suppose it's human nature not to want to look at what lurks beneath the pretty candy coating. I know there are people who exhibit the same duplicity. They're beautiful and full of life on the outside, but dark and devoid of a soul beneath the surface."

"Those are the people who hurt you the most," Naomi agreed.

I turned and looked to the spot on the little knoll where Naomi seemed to stand. "Is that what happened to you? Did someone you trusted hurt you?"

Naomi began to fade away.

"Don't go," I breathed. "I'm not going to hurt you. No one is ever going to hurt you again. I promise."

Naomi's image grew stronger. The music began to fade, but just a bit.

"That's a beautiful song. Is it something you learned to play?"

Naomi moved toward the spot where Tucker was sleeping. He didn't stir when she knelt down beside him. "It's a song Mr. Kline taught me. I don't remember the name, but it was playing in the background when..." Naomi faded again.

"It's all right," I said encouragingly. "I'm here to help. You're safe now."

After a moment, she appeared. I didn't want to send her running back to wherever it was she waited in the void, but I needed to ask. "Do you remember what happened? Do you remember how you ended up in the grave?"

Naomi shook her head. "No. I can't remember anything after the car."

"The car?" I asked.

"Mama went away. I was scared of what was going to happen. Papa didn't seem to care that she was gone. I think he was just as happy without her. It didn't seem right not to care about the woman you were married to, but he said she was sick, and things would be better without her. I thought I understood what he meant."

"Were things better?" I asked.

Naomi shook her head. "Not really. It was nice not to have to worry about Mama's spells, Papa was in a better mood. But he still drank a lot, and he still carried on with Mrs. Woodbine the way a married man shouldn't. I tried to pretend I couldn't hear what they were doing, but the walls in the house were thin and Mrs. Woodbine was loud."

I cringed. The poor girl. No one should have to witness their father's infidelity. "Did you say anything to your father about what you heard?"

"I tried to once, but he said I was bad for listening. He sent me to my room. After that, I started going out when Mrs. Woodbine came over."

"Where did you go?" I asked.

"Just out. I didn't have friends, but I knew some people. Mostly I went to Mr. Kline's. I liked to play his piano, and he let me when Jane wasn't there. She didn't like me. I heard her say it wasn't right that he let me come over when he was alone, but he said it was his house and his life, and he'd do what he wanted with both."

I suddenly wondered if it hadn't been Jane Smith, the colleague turned wife, who was responsible for Naomi's death. "Did you ever speak to Jane or spend time with her?"

"No. She didn't like me. She thought it was me Mr. Kline had feelings for, but he didn't. Still, he sent me away when she was around."

"You said the last thing you remembered was the car," I prompted.

Naomi hung her head. "Mrs. Woodbine came to visit, and Papa was drunk. I knew things weren't going to be good at home, so I went over to Mr. Kline's. He said he was getting ready to go out. He said I could come back the next day if I wanted to. I didn't want to go home and I had nowhere else to go, so I snuck into Mr. Kline's car and hid in the backseat. I was scared and sorry as we drove south. Papa would say it was the craziness I'd inherited from Mama that made me do such a stupid thing. I guess he would have been right. I knew Mr. Kline was going to be mad if he found me hiding. I was afraid he wouldn't let me come over anymore. I was afraid he'd stop teaching me to play the piano."

"What happened?" I asked. "Did he find you?"

Naomi squinted and rubbed her brow. "I don't know. I don't remember. I remember riding in the car. I remember the song playing in the CD player. I remember being scared. But I don't remember anything after that." Naomi faded away.

"Okay. It's okay," I said softly. "We don't need to remember everything today. Can I come back tomorrow?"

Naomi appeared once again. "Okay. Can you bring the dog?"

"I can. I have a cat too. Shadow. Do you like cats?"

Naomi nodded. This time when she disappeared, she didn't come back.

I called Tucker to my side.

Mr. Kline was beginning to look more and more like Naomi's killer, although, as odd as it seemed, I suspected Naomi was lying to me.

Chapter 10

Mac was sitting on the back deck talking on her cell when Tucker and I got home. After greeting Sunny, who was all wagging tail, sloppy kisses, and excited yips, I grabbed a bottle of water from the refrigerator and joined her. She held up a finger, indicating that she'd be just a minute. I opened my water, took a sip, and then leaned my forearms against the railing to look out over the calm, clear sea. I wasn't sure who Mac was talking to, but it sounded like a business call. When Mac set out to do something, she went all in; judging by the long hours she'd put in since she'd arrived, I was willing to bet her software company was going to take the technology world by storm.

"That was Ty," Mac informed me after she hung up.

"Ty?" I asked.

"Tyson Matthews. He's a techy like me, only way ahead of me in know-how, at least at this point."

"He's going to help you start your business?" I'd heard enough of the conversation to know Mac had asked him for a favor.

"Yes, if I need it. But that wasn't why I called him. I asked him if he could find out anything about Bodine Collins. I don't know if there's anything Woody doesn't already know, but I thought we could dig around a bit. Collins isn't going to give us anything voluntarily."

"You're pretty good at digging stuff up on people," I said. "Why bring in anyone else?"

Mac shrugged. "For one thing, I don't have all my equipment set up yet. And I hadn't had the chance to let Ty know about my move, so it was a good opportunity to fill him in."

I glanced at Mac, who was trying very hard not to look directly at me. "You like him. And not just in a fellow nerd sort of way. You're really in to him."

Mac blushed. "We're just friends, but yeah. He does push all the right buttons. He's not only brilliant but he's good-looking and ridiculously nice."

"Does he live in California?"

"No. Portland."

I raised a brow. "You don't say. I don't suppose that's really why you decided to leave the tech capital of the country and start your new business here in tiny Cutter's Cove?"

"I can do what I do from anywhere, so I decided to come back to Cutter's Cove to be close to Trev, and you too."

"You didn't know I was staying when you made the move," I pointed out.

"Okay, I moved back to Cutter's Cove to be close to Trevor."

"Uh-huh," I said with a big grin on my face.

Mac ran her hands through her hair. "It's not a big deal."

"I never said it was."

"Okay, then. How did your meet and greet with Naomi go?"

Mac was trying very hard to change the subject, and I decided I'd let her. In a way, it seemed strange to see Mac get so flustered over a guy. She wasn't a kid anymore, and I knew she'd had boyfriends, but she'd shared with me that her dating life was pretty sparse because she preferred to spend Friday nights with her computer rather than random guys. I couldn't wait to meet the man who'd generated a ruffled state in my otherwise unflappable friend.

"Naomi made an appearance today. She said she didn't remember how she died or who killed her, but she remembered stowing away in Jeffrey Kline's car." I reminded her who he was, then told her everything Naomi had shared with me. "Oh, and Woody uncovered some information about Kline as well."

"So, if Naomi remembered stowing away in Kline's car he would have had to be in town when she died."

"Most likely. The real problem is that, at this point at least, her memories are blurry and incomplete. Unless she can put dates to them, I'm not sure we can make a case against him. For all we know, she stowed away in Kline's car weeks before she went missing. I'm going back tomorrow. I hope if we talk it out, the details of her last hours will begin to emerge."

"That poor girl. It hurts my heart to even imagine what she must have gone through."

"Yes," I agreed. "This is a tough one. I'm glad I have you and Trev to share it with. We still on for tonight?"

"Still on. Trevor said we should meet him at his place, and it's fine to bring the dogs if we want. He's going to build a fire in the fire pit he built into his deck. He has deck heaters as well, but sometimes a cold breeze blows in off the water. He recommended we dress in layers. Oh, and he has wine and a cheese tray, but if we were inclined to pick up something chocolate he wouldn't mind."

"I'll make brownies," I offered. "Trev loves brownies."

"He also said your mom was welcome to come, but she hasn't left the attic all day, so I'm thinking she might be otherwise occupied."

I relaxed back into a deck chair. "It's been a long time since I've seen her paint with such fervor. It's great to see her so passionate, but I hope she doesn't overdo. I might try to get her out for a while tomorrow. Maybe take her on a photography expedition. She wanted some photos of the marina and the wharf. Maybe we can have lunch there. You're welcome to join us if you'd like."

"I might. I'll see how things go."

"I want to go back to talk to Naomi again too. I might go early. I doubt she cares if I show up at the crack of dawn."

"I assume ghosts don't sleep."

I thought of Alyson and how it had been for her while she waited for me for ten long years. When I showed up she'd been happy to see me, but I didn't get the sense her time alone had been unmanageable. I wondered, now that we were joined—assuming we were for good—if she had a separate consciousness or if her sense of self had merged with mine. I realized I really did want to be sure she was okay. That she was as happy as I was. Chan had made things sound pretty simple and straightforward, but I didn't find anything simple or straightforward about having part of yourself suddenly appear as a separate entity and then disappear just as abruptly.

I needed walnuts for the brownies, so I'd have to go into town anyway. Perhaps I'd go to the magic shop to have another chat with Chan while I was there.

******

Unfortunately, the shop was closed when I stopped by. According to the sign that was always on the window, Chan was open when he was open and closed when he wasn't. I wasn't sure how he could run a business that way, but he'd owned the shop for a lot of years, so it must work for him. It was possible he had plans for the weekend. I could stop by again on Monday to speak to him about Alyson.

From there, I headed to the market. While I'd been able to avoid the tricky situation until this point, I knew eventually I'd run into someone who knew me as Alyson but didn't know about my time in witness protection.

"Alyson, is that you?" Stephanie Nelson chirped as I went through the store to the nut section.

"Stephanie, how are you? I'm actually going by Amanda now, but yes, it's me."

She frowned. "You changed your name?"

I'd picked a white lie to use for people who remembered me but weren't close-enough friends to be given the long, true explanation. "Alyson is my middle name. I'd decided to try it out when I lived in Cutter's Cove as a teen. My first name is Amanda, and I went back to it."

"I see," she said, though her expression indicated she didn't. "So, are you here for a visit?"

"Actually, I've decided to move back."

Stephanie leaned on her half-full grocery basket. "I wondered if perhaps your family didn't still own the house on the bluff. No one has lived there since you left."

I nodded. "My mother still owns it. So, how have you been? Did you and Art Hollister end up getting married?"

"Yes, we did. We have three beautiful children. Art works for the public utility district and I teach preschool three mornings a week. How about you? Married?"

"No, still single."

"So, have you been living in New York all this time?"

"I have, but I felt it was time to come back. I'm looking forward to a slower pace."

Stephanie brushed her dark hair away from her face. She looked the same as she had in high school, except for the fatigue in her eyes. I imagined having three kids would do that to you. "Are you still planning to solve mysteries the way you did when you lived here before?" she asked.

"I didn't solve any mysteries in New York, but the reason I came back to Cutter's Cove in the first place was to look into Rory Oswald's death."

Stephanie put a manicured hand on my arm. "Wasn't that just so tragic?"

"It was," I agreed.

She gave my arm a little squeeze. "Well, I'm glad you're back. You seemed to have a knack for solving crimes. Not that Cutter's Cove has a lot of crime, but every town has some. I heard Officer Baker has been talking to people about a girl who's been missing since before you lived here the first time. You should talk to him about it. He might be happy for the help."

"Actually, I have spoken to him about it. I don't suppose you remember Naomi Collins?"

Stephanie shook her head. "Not me, but my older sister Isabelle was in the same class with her all through school."

"Did Isabelle have any idea what might have happened to her?" I asked, then stepped aside to allow a young mother with two toddlers and a full basket to pass.

Stephanie leaned in and lowered her voice. "Isabelle said if Naomi was murdered, which is the current rumor, it was probably her mother or father who killed her." She leaned in even closer. "You know her dad was a drunk and her mom was as loony as they came? Isabelle thought either could have had a fit and smacked the girl one time too many."

"Are you saying Naomi's mother hit her the same as her father?"

Stephanie nodded. "Isabelle remembered her mother coming to school when they were in the fourth or fifth grade. Isabelle had been out with a bathroom pass and saw Naomi leave the classroom with her mother and followed. The mother had her by the arm, dragging her to the place behind the cafeteria where all the bad kids hung out at recess. When Isabelle came around the corner, she saw the mother was shaking her and yelling at her. Naomi was crying and saying she didn't do it, whatever it was, but it was like her mother totally lost it. She was shaking her so hard, Isabelle was afraid she was going to shake Naomi to death. Isabelle was about to go find a teacher when suddenly the mother stopped what she was doing and started hugging Naomi, saying she was sorry. She kept saying she didn't mean it and it would never happen again. Naomi was still crying, but when her mother let her go, she stood there like a statue, which Isabelle thought was dumb."

"Dumb why?" I asked.

"Isabelle said if someone was shaking her like that and then let her go, she'd run away, but Naomi just stood there as if she was used to it and knew running wouldn't do any good."

"And then what happened?"

"Naomi went into the bathroom, washed her face, and went back to class as if nothing had happened."

I thought back to my conversation with Amelia Collins Landry. She'd admitted to being crazy and having a spell that landed her in the mental facility where she'd been at the time Naomi disappeared. She'd also told me they'd done tests that somehow didn't come out right. I wondered if she'd had periodic episodes of rage. I thanked Stephanie for welcoming me home and sharing what she knew, bought my nuts, and headed toward the police station to tell Woody. Luckily, he was often there even when he wasn't officially working.

"Two visits in one day. To what do I owe this honor?" Woody greeted me as I walked in.

"Just a short one this time," I promised. "I was at the grocery store and ran into an old acquaintance. She told me a story she'd heard from her older sister about Naomi and her mother from when the two of them were in grade school. Naomi's mother was sent to a mental health facility after having an episode that supposedly happened when she found her husband in bed with another woman. I've been operating under the assumption that her attack on Mrs. Woodbine was an isolated event, but my friend's sister saw her dragging Naomi out of school years before and shaking her so hard she was afraid she was going to kill her."

Woody frowned. "You're suggesting Naomi was being abused by both her parents?"

"Maybe. It sounds to me as if Naomi's father might have been just a jerk, while the episode with her mother was much more than that. Maybe Mrs. Collins had a psychotic break of some sort. I don't know whether something like that was a frequent occurrence, but it seems like it's worth looking in to."

"I agree. I'll see what I can find out."

"When I spoke to Naomi's mother, she told me she'd been sent to the facility because she'd had some tests after attacking Mrs. Woodbine that hadn't come out right. I don't suppose it would be possible to get a look at that information?"

"Not without a court order, and we'd need a whole lot more than we have to get one. We'd need evidence to suggest Naomi's mother was the one who killed her. And that would be impossible, because she was already in the mental health facility when Naomi disappeared."

I sighed. "That's true. I don't suppose Naomi's mother can be considered a suspect. Still, I'd be interested in finding out who was responsible for Naomi's bruises while she was growing up."

Chapter 11

Trevor was waiting for Mac and me when we arrived at his house. He had a warm fire going in the pit, wine open and sitting with glasses on the outdoor table, baskets of fruit, sliced baguettes, and crackers, and a tray with both hard and soft cheeses, as well as several kinds of spread. I found myself happy I'd only had a sandwich for dinner; everything looked delicious.

Mac and I sat down on a couple of comfortable chairs around the fire. It was a warm evening and the air was still, so the patio heaters weren't necessary. The waves crashing onto the shore just beyond the sand gave the evening the same sensation as one of the beach parties we'd attended when we were teenagers.

"Now *this*," I said, as I settled into my cushioned seat with a plate of cheese and a glass of wine, "is the life."

"I love it here," Trevor said, "though I sometimes wish I had the isolation you do up on the bluff. There aren't a lot of beachgoers out tonight, but in July and August it can get pretty crowded. While still beautiful, it's less relaxing when there are people walking back and forth between you and the water."

"I guess that would get old fast. And summer days must be even worse," I said.

"I don't mind the daytime crowd so much, but I spend my time in my workshop on the busiest evenings." Trevor turned his head slightly. "So, Mac, how goes the move and the business?"

"As for the move, Amanda allowing me to move in with her has made that a lot easier than I anticipated."

"I'm happy for the company," I said.

Mac smiled. "Me too. As for the business, it will take a while to get it up and running. I'm in the process of letting my clients know about the change. I'll need to figure out exactly where I want to focus my energy, but I have a ton of ideas. I just have to narrow things down and focus in."

"The company you recently worked for specializes in business software, doesn't it?" I asked.

Mac nodded. "Business software for large corporations. My real interest is cybersecurity, but I have a reputation in business software, so, in the short term at least, I think my best bet might be to develop that, for smaller companies. Maybe even for home businesses. I can always expand into cybersecurity, but getting larger corporations to take a chance on a startup would be a challenge. I had a long chat with my friend Ty. He thought we might be able to team up on a few concepts he's been working on for security linked to social media. I of course couldn't commit without looking at the nuts and bolts of his idea, but teaming up on a project or two might be a good way for me to build my own brand."

"And to spend time with the guy you've been crushing on for years," Trevor teased.

"I haven't been crushing on anyone. Ty and I are just friends," Mac insisted.

"Tomorrow's my Sunday off," Trevor informed us. "I thought we could do something together."

I stretched my legs out in front of me. "I thought you were only closed on Mondays."

"I am, but my manager and I take turns taking Sundays off. So, how about it? Do you want to go surfing? Antiquing? I can even borrow a sailboat if a day on the water is more to your liking."

"I'd love to spend the day with just the three of us," Mac said, "but I didn't know you were going to be off, so I made plans to go to Portland to see Ty. How about Monday? And I vote for surfing. I'm not really in to antiques, and you know I get seasick in sailboats."

Trevor looked at me. "Amanda?"

"I'd love to go antiquing tomorrow, and I'd welcome a chance to spend Monday on the beach with both of you. I'll want to go by to try to make a connection with Naomi, so maybe we can pay her a visit while we're out."

"Works for me," Trevor said. "How are things going with the investigation?"

I filled him in about my brief encounter with Naomi and my two conversations with Woody. "If Stephanie's sister is right, and Naomi's mother was prone to acts of rage even before she attacked Mrs.

Woodbine, I'd add her to the suspect list, but we know she was at the mental health facility before Naomi went missing, so it couldn't have been her."

"Well," Mac said, "that isn't completely true."

I raised a brow. "Do you know something I don't?"

Mac set her wineglass down on a nearby table. "I spoke to Ty again while you were in the shower. If you remember, I asked him to look into Bodine Collins, which he did, but he looked into his wife as well. Although it was tricky, he managed to hack into Amelia Collins's admittance and residence records at the mental health facility. While researching Naomi's father, Ty developed a hunch about Mrs. Collins that, as it turns out, might tell us something."

"What did he discover?" I asked.

"Although the testing was requested by the courts, after receiving the results, Mrs. Collins agreed to be admitted to the facility voluntarily. Her time there began three weeks before Naomi went missing. Ty learned that self-admitted patients are allowed short off-campus visits after the two-week point. According to her file, Mrs. Collins was checked out twice between the time she was first admitted and the time Naomi disappeared."

"For how long?" I asked.

"Two hours each time. She was picked up by a friend and dropped back at the facility later."

I felt my stomach knot. "Do we know which friend?"

"Jeffrey Kline."

I put my hand to my throat as it tightened. I felt as if I couldn't breathe. Suddenly, a theory I didn't want to consider filtered into my mind. "Naomi told me that she went to see Mr. Kline when Mrs. Woodbine came to see her father. Kline told her that he couldn't see her that day and suggested she come back the next. Naomi didn't want to go home and snuck into the backseat of his car. What if Kline was going to see Naomi's mother? What if somewhere along the way, Naomi was discovered in the backseat? What if it turned out Kline and Mrs. Collins were having an affair, and now the cat was out of the bag, causing a ruckus? What if Naomi was pushed or fell and hit her head?"

Mac put a hand to her mouth. "You think her mother might have killed her?"

I shrugged. "Maybe, if she went into one of her rages. Or maybe it was Kline who killed her, and Mrs. Collins covered up for him."

"While the idea has possibilities, it seems like kind of a long shot," Trevor said. "We know Kline was single when Naomi went missing. Why would he care if an affair became public knowledge? People knew Naomi's father was cheating on his wife. Why would she care if it got out that she was cheating on him?"

"I'm not sure," I admitted. "But there has to be more to this. I've maintained all along that whoever buried Naomi cared about her. The only suspects until now who cared about her were Naomi's father and Jeffrey Kline. Until just now, I couldn't take Naomi's mother seriously as a suspect, but if she was with Kline that day, and he was her lover, and she found Naomi in the backseat of his car, maybe the betrayal caused her to go crazy, the same way she had with Mrs. Woodbine."

"How can we know?" Mac asked.

"I have to find a way to get Naomi to remember. If her mother is the one who killed her, it would be natural for her to want to suppress it."

******

Later that night, I stood in front of my bedroom window and looked out at the sea. I found I actually hoped to have the dream that had been playing havoc with my sleep tonight in the hope of picking up some new piece of the puzzle, but with all the theories playing in my head, I'd been unable to sleep a wink. I really didn't want Naomi's mother—or her father, for that matter—to be responsible for her death, but I'd suspected almost from the beginning that someone she loved, and who loved her back, had been her killer. The thought of such a betrayal tore at my heart, leaving me feeling raw, exposed, and vulnerable, even as I'd allowed myself to bond with the girl whose death I hoped to avenge. Could Naomi have known what had happened to her all along? Could she be covering for the people she continued to love even after they ended her life? On that first day she connected with me, she'd been certain Jeffrey Kline hadn't hurt her. How could she know that with such certainty unless she knew who *had* hurt her?

Despite it being the middle of the night, I felt an overwhelming urge to go to Naomi. To talk to her and try to help her to understand that it seemed to move on, she needed to help me uncover the facts surrounding her death. I knew I was probably crazy even as I pulled on a pair of jeans and a sweatshirt. Slipping my feet into tennis shoes, I grabbed Shadow and headed downstairs.

I considered taking the dogs but decided to leave them at the last minute. I jotted down a note for my mother, should she awaken and wonder where I was, then went out into the dark night. I didn't pass a single car as I made the drive south. When I arrived at the parking area, I clicked on my flashlight and called for Shadow to follow.

The stars overhead papered the night sky with bursts of light that made me think of fairy dust. I paused and looked up as I reached the top of the knoll where Naomi had been buried. I looked for the constellations I'd memorized the first time I'd lived in Cutter's Cove and saw again how breathtaking the sky was when there were no lights to distract from their brilliance.

"Naomi," I whispered. Shadow sat at my feet and waited. "It's Amanda. I want to talk to you. Can you hear me? Are you here?"

I stood perfectly still as I waited. The waves crashed in the distance and still I waited for the music that preceded her arrival.

"There's no need to be afraid," I said. "I just want to talk to you. And I brought my cat."

A gentle breeze brushed my face as I listened for the music. I sensed that Naomi was nearby, but despite my best efforts, I couldn't quite lure her out of hiding. "You can trust me, Naomi," I said into the night sky. "I'm here to help you. I won't hurt you."

I closed my eyes and let the sound of the surf, the scent of the sea, and the moisture in the air envelop me. I felt myself falling into my own thoughts as the slightest hint of music began to roll in from another dimension. Shadow moved away from my side. I could feel Naomi's presence, so I dared to open my eyes. Naomi shimmered before me. Not fully visible, yet identifiable.

"I'm glad you came," I said in a soft voice.

Naomi looked down at the cat. Her image grew brighter as she knelt to pet him. I didn't know what sort of magic allowed Shadow to see and interact with spirits, but I had found his offer of comfort to those I attempted to help invaluable.

"I hoped we could continue our conversation," I began. "Your story of the night you snuck into Mr. Kline's car."

"I have to go," Naomi said as she began to fade.

"Wait. I want to help."

"You don't understand."

"I do," I insisted, even though deep in my soul I knew I couldn't. "I want to. I know you were hurt. Betrayed. I know you want to protect the person who hurt you. That's natural. But I also know it's only in sharing what happened that you'll be set free."

Naomi didn't answer. I was losing her. Somehow, I knew if she left me tonight, she'd never reappear. I needed help. I needed Alyson. Then suddenly, as if my wish alone could bring her forth, she appeared.

"It wasn't right," Alyson said to Naomi, whose image had once again grown brighter. "You needed him, but it was your mother he went to that night. It was always your mother he went to."

"They didn't think I knew," Naomi whispered. "All those times she snuck out of the house and went to him."

"You loved him," Alyson said. "But he loved her."

Naomi drifted away, but Alyson followed. I simply stood and watched. Eventually, Naomi began to speak. "I didn't mean to make problems. I just wanted to be with him. Talk to him. Find a safe place to be while Papa was with Mrs. Woodbine. Mr. Kline told me he had to go, but I didn't want to be alone, so I snuck into the backseat. I hoped he'd smile when he found me. I hoped he'd see how much I wanted to be with him. But he wanted to be with her. He always wanted to be with her."

If Naomi's mother was having an affair with Mr. Kline and Naomi's father was having an affair with Mrs. Woodbine, why did they stay married? Why not divorce and move on to live separate yet most likely happier lives?

"You were so angry when he picked her up at the facility," Alyson continued.

Naomi nodded.

"It wasn't right. You needed him, but he went to her."

"It wasn't his fault. He didn't know," Naomi said. "He tried to help me, but Mama was so mad that I'd snuck into the car. She didn't mean to hurt me. She couldn't help it when she had one of her spells. Papa said she didn't mean it."

"She shook you," I realized. "The way she did in the past. She shook you to try to make you understand."

"It was my fault," Naomi whispered. "I shouldn't have made Mama mad. Papa said it was important not to make Mama mad. I should have known he would go to her."

"She pushed you and you fell," I said.

"It was an accident."

"You hit your head," I continued.

"Mr. Kline tried to help me. He held me in his arms and tried to stop the bleeding, but there was so much. Too much."

"So he buried you on the little knoll overlooking the sea," I finished.

"He said he was sorry. He said he'd come back to visit, but he never did. I've been waiting, but he hasn't come."

Suddenly, I realized Naomi's unfinished business, the chain that bound her to the earthly plane, wasn't that her own mother had killed her. It was the promise of a visit from the man she loved that held her here.

"He won't come," Alyson said.

"He promised." And Naomi was gone.

Shadow wound his way through my legs. I bent and picked him up. "Alyson?" I called, but she was gone too, vanished as abruptly as she'd appeared. If nothing else, I now knew that while ghost me might have reintegrated with me, she still had her own form and identity. At least for now.

I let out a breath as the enormity of what had happened to Naomi gripped me. I'd found out what had happened to her but had no way to prove it. I'd failed in my attempt to help Naomi move on because solving her murder had never been the point. What could I do now?

Chapter 12

Sunday, June 17

By the time Shadow and I made it home, the sky had just begun to lighten. I made a cup of coffee and went out onto the deck. My heart was heavy with the responsibility I felt toward Naomi, combined with the realization that I had no idea how to help her. I could tell Woody what I'd found out and he could follow up. If either Naomi's mother or Mr. Kline confessed to their part in Naomi's death, at least that part of the situation would be resolved, although it seemed for Naomi to really move on she needed Jeffrey Kline to follow through with his promise and return to the grave where he'd left the troubled young girl who had placed all her happiness at his feet.

"You're up early," Mac said as she sat down beside me.

"I never went to bed," I answered. "Or at least I never went to sleep. I tried to go to bed, but I couldn't sleep."

"Naomi?"

I nodded. "I went to see her."

"And…?"

"It was her mother who killed her. Not intentionally. At least, I don't think it was intentional. She pushed Naomi, which made her fall and hit her head."

Mac frowned. "How sad."

"Actually," I sighed, "what's really sad is that it was Mr. Kline who buried her. He promised to come back to visit. It's Mr. Kline she's waiting for. If he doesn't come, she won't move on."

"What are you going to do?"

I closed my eyes and let out a heartfelt sigh as fatigue and helplessness gripped my body. "I have no idea."

Mac and I sat quietly as the enormity of the situation weighed on our minds. The sun began its brilliant ascent into the sky, but I didn't even notice. My responsibility to Naomi couldn't be fulfilled until I enabled her to move on; despite the seeming impossibility, I had to find a way. I supposed the first thing I should do was share what I knew with Woody. I didn't have any proof to give him, of course, other than my word that a ghost had told me a story under the stars near a grave by the sea.

At some point, Mac went inside to get ready for her trip to Portland and Trevor arrived for our day of antiquing. I told him I still wanted to spend the day with him, but I'd come to the realization that I needed to try to reach out to Naomi's mother. I'd want

Woody to arrest Naomi's mother and Jeffrey Kline immediately after I told them what I'd learned, but he wouldn't be able to do it unless I could give him the proof he needed. The only thing I could do was go to Amelia Collins Landry and somehow get her to confess.

******

"Thanks for coming with me," I said to Trevor later that morning as we made the drive south again.

"You know I'm happy to help. But do you really think you can get Naomi's mother to confess to killing her?"

I slid back beside Trevor in the driver's seat. "I don't know. I think she loved her daughter despite the abuse she doled out for most of her life. It appears she really did, possibly still does suffer from a mental illness that I suppose could explain the abuse. It must bother her to know what she's done and not be able to talk to anyone about it. If it were me in her situation, I might be just as happy to confess."

"She has to know admitting to what she did will land her in prison."

"Maybe. But I'd think punishment for crimes committed would be easier to endure than internal punishment for sins not confessed."

I hadn't called ahead this time; I was afraid she would refuse to see me, so I'd decided to show up and take my chances that she'd be home. It was Sunday so there was a good possibility her new family would be there as well. I considered waiting until the next day, but now that I knew the truth, I needed to get this over with. If I could get her to confess, maybe I could

153

convince Mr. Kline he had nothing to lose by keeping the promise he'd made to Naomi all those years ago.

When we arrived at the house I'd visited once before, we found Amelia Collins Landry in the front yard, tending a bed of annuals. Trevor pulled up to the side and parked. The woman looked up when we both climbed out of the vehicle. I could see her tense, as if she was considering darting away, but Trevor, with his long legs, reached her before she had the chance to flee.

"What are you doing here?" she asked nervously. "I agreed to speak to you that one time, but you can't just show up whenever you want. What if my husband was here? What would he say if he knew you were snooping around, digging up things best left buried?"

"Your husband knows about Naomi?" I asked. "He knows you killed her?"

Her eyes grew wide. "Who said I killed her? I didn't kill her. It was an accident. A very tragic accident. It was Jeffrey, wasn't it? You talked to Jeffrey and he told you everything. I knew I couldn't trust him. He said he'd take care of everything, but I knew I couldn't trust him."

"If it really was an accident, as you claim, I think you should have a chance to tell your side of the story," I said, skirting the Jeffrey Kline issue. "I have a friend, Woody Baker, who'll be willing to listen to what you have to say. He might be able to help you."

"Is this Woody?" She nodded to Trevor.

"No. This is Trevor. Woody is a police officer."

Fear slipped quietly into her eyes. "A cop? We can't tell a cop. Jeffrey said we shouldn't. He said it was an accident. He said he'd take care of everything."

I nodded at Trevor. This was his cue to call Woody and tell him to join us right away. I figured if he turned on his siren, he could be here in less than thirty minutes. I just needed to keep her talking until then. I clicked on my phone to record what she said. I wasn't sure about the rules regarding the admissibility of a confession recorded without the suspect's consent, but if she finally told the story she'd been hiding for sixteen years, I didn't want to miss a word of it, even if it couldn't be used in court.

"Jeffrey came to pick you up," I said. "He didn't know Naomi was in the backseat of his car," I continued after Trevor had walked away to make the call. "She wasn't supposed to be there."

"She was hiding. I didn't mean for her to see. To know what Jeffrey and I had been doing. It was wrong and sinful. It's a parent's duty to shield their child from such things."

"I understand your desire to protect her. I imagine she was upset when she saw the two of you together."

She nodded. "She was so angry. I could see the rage in her eyes. She kept yelling at me, screaming that he was hers. I tried to make her understand she was just a child and he could never be hers, but she was very angry."

"So the two of you struggled?"

Huge tears welled up in Amelia's eyes. "I tried to calm her down. I grabbed her arms and held on tight. I tried to shake the devil out of her, but she wouldn't let me. She was too angry. She had the craziness in her, same as me. She tried to pull free, but I held on tight. I'm strong, but I guess somewhere along the

155

way she'd grown stronger. She twisted and pulled away. She jerked herself out of my grip and turned to run. As she turned, she tripped on something, I think a log, or maybe a rock. She screamed and started to fall. She hit the ground hard. So hard. Jeffrey tried to help her, but there was too much blood. So very much blood. I guess I went a little crazy. I don't remember a lot after that. Jeffrey told me he'd take care of everything. He told me I needed to calm down, but I couldn't, so he gave me a pill that would do it. I guess he drove me back to the facility. I don't remember that part of it. I remember Naomi falling. I remember the blood. But the next thing I knew for sure was waking up in my bed."

"Did you see Jeffrey again after that day?"

She nodded. "He came by the facility to tell me that he was leaving Cutter's Cove. He said it would be for the best for both of us. I hated to see him go, but I was a married woman and he was single. I knew he was right. I'd made an oath to my husband. I'd broken that oath. His leaving was my punishment."

"Did he tell you what he'd done with Naomi's body?" I asked.

"He said she was happy with the angels. He said she was in a beautiful place. That she could finally find the peace she'd been looking for all her life."

"And after that?" I asked.

"I did my therapy. I took my pills. I got better. I've had some hard times since Naomi left us, but I got better." She looked at me. "Is your friend going to put me in jail?"

"I don't know. Maybe," I answered honestly, just as I saw Woody's cruiser pull up to the curb.

She hung her head. "It's for the best. There are some secrets that should be kept, but this is one that needed to be told."

Chapter 13

Monday, June 25

"This table has to be mine," I said to Trevor a week later. We'd never made it antiquing the day Naomi's mother confessed to her part in her daughter's death, but Trevor had given me a rain check.

"It would look good in your entry," Trev agreed. "Although it needs some work. I can handle the repairs, but we'll want to negotiate on the price."

"Why? I can afford the asking price and I want it."

Trevor grinned. "Negotiating is part of the process. I take it you aren't used to bartering."

"Too stressful."

"Maybe for you, but negotiating is my superpower. In fact, I'm known in some circles as

Negotiator Man. You wouldn't want to rob me of my chance to save the day by saving you a few bucks."

There he was, my goofy friend Trev. The prank-playing comic-book junkie who'd befriended me in high school. "No, bargaining over prices isn't my thing, but if you enjoy the give and take, go for it." I looked around the shop. "While you're doing that, I'm going to check out that umbrella stand. It would be a perfect accompaniment to the table."

When Trevor had first suggested antiquing I'd said I'd go, but I wasn't sure I'd like rooting around items that had been discarded by others for one reason or another, but damn if it wasn't a blast. The past week had been stressful, and I welcomed a day of eating, shopping, and fun. Mac was in Portland with Ty, again, and Mom had taken a trip down the coast to do some shopping of her own in San Francisco. Neither Mom nor Mac would be home until the following day, so I hadn't been sure what to do about the dogs, but Woody had offered to come by to let them out at midday, and I decided to let him. He was a responsible guy, and Trevor and I would be back in time for sunset and dinner.

I hadn't seen Alyson again after that day on the bluff, but for the first time since I'd decided to stay in Cutter's Cove, I felt confident she was close by and happy. The only dark spot on my otherwise perfect life was that I suspected Naomi was still waiting for Jeffrey Kline to return, something, I felt sure, would never happen. Both Amelia Collins Landry and Kline had been arrested for their part in Naomi's death and its cover-up. There were some extenuating circumstances and I wasn't sure how things would work out, but that was up to the district attorney and courts.

"Blue or gray?" Trevor asked.

"Blue or gray what?" I asked.

"I found a frame for your bed. I think you'll love it, but it'll need to be refinished. Do you want me to paint it blue or gray?"

I lifted a brow. "Can I see it before I commit?"

"Absolutely."

Trevor took me by the arm and led me across the large warehouse-size building. I hadn't mentioned it to Trevor yet, but I'd already picked out a frame from a catalog after he mentioned that the bed I'd bought as a teen needed a new frame that was better suited to my new life as an adult living in that room. I hadn't ordered it yet, but I planned to. Still, Trevor was being such a sweetie that I felt I owed it to him to at least take a look at what he'd found.

"What do you think?"

I put my hand over my heart when I saw the large metal frame with its intricate design. It was old, unique, and perfect. "It's fantastic."

Trevor beamed. "You really like it?"

I nodded. "I do. It's the most perfect thing I never knew I wanted. Until now, of course. Now I have to have it."

"It'll need work, but I think it's going to be just right in your room. So blue or gray?"

"Blue. Dark blue. A full, rich blue. It'll really stand out against the gray walls."

Trevor headed over to find the owner of the antique barn to negotiate a price, while I stepped outside for some fresh air. I was having the best day, but I hoped to hear from Woody, who'd promised to try to arrange a visit by Jeffrey to Naomi's gravesite as part of whatever deal they were working out. I felt my heart break just a bit when I saw the text from Woody informing me that Jeffrey had refused to take the deal in its entirety, which meant he was going to be tried.

"We should go talk to her again." Alyson suddenly appeared.

"You think she'll listen to us?"

She shrugged. "She might. Then again, she might not. It's worth a shot."

I took a deep breath. "Okay. As soon as Trevor gets back from trying to knock a few bucks off the furniture I'm buying."

"I like the bed frame," Alyson said. "It's different but just right."

I smiled. "It is just right. I'm pretty sure I walked past it the first time, but once Trev pointed it out, I knew I had to have it."

Alyson faded away as Trevor walked out. "All set," he said. "I just need to load your purchases into my truck and we can head down the road to the next stop on the Trevor Johnson Antiques Roadshow."

"I'd like to stop by to try to talk to Naomi. I don't know if I can get through to her, but we aren't far from the burial site and I need to try."

Trevor took my hand in his. "Are you sure? I hate to see that sunny smile turn to sadness."

"I'm sure."

"Okay. Then let me load the truck and we'll head over."

Alyson appeared just as Trevor walked away. She took my hand in hers. "Don't worry. We'll do this together. I know Naomi wants to be happy. We just need to make her see that she can be."

When we arrived at the bluff, I told Trevor that Alyson was with me and it might be best if he waited for us in the truck. He agreed to do so without saying a word about it. That was one of the things I liked best about spending time with Trevor: everything was so easy. Ethan had liked to discuss things. To debate. Yes, even to negotiate. Perhaps that came from being an attorney, but, as I said, it wasn't something I enjoyed.

My stomach knotted and churned as I walked along the dirt path to the little hill where Naomi had been laid to rest. I wondered if her father was planning to rebury her now that he had what was left of her. I supposed someone would bury her remains somewhere. I made a mental note to check on that. If her parents didn't take the initiative to find a lovely spot for her final resting place, I would.

Alyson joined me as soon as we reached our destination. I paused and called Naomi's name. She didn't appear at first, but after a while I heard the music.

"Did you bring him?" Naomi asked.

"No," I answered truthfully. "I tried, but I'm not sure it's going to work out. He did send a message for you."

Naomi looked hesitant. "A message?"

Alyson stepped forward. She took Naomi's hand in hers. "Mr. Kline wants you to know that he cares about you. He wants you to be happy. He wants you to move on."

"But..."

Alyson touched Naomi's translucent face with her translucent hand. "It's time. He's of this world and you aren't. You can never be together. Not the way you want. The only way to set him free of his obligation to you is for you to move on to the next phase of your existence."

"I'm scared."

Alyson held out her hand. "I'll come with you partway."

Now I wanted to argue. The last thing I needed was to be pulled into some afterlife dimension, but Alyson sent me a look asking me to trust her, so I did. I watched as both figures faded away. I hoped Naomi would find in the afterlife what she never had in life. Love. Acceptance. Joy. After a few minutes, Alyson reappeared. "It's done. Can we go home now?"

I nodded, then watched as Alyson's form melted into mine.

Next From Kathi Daley Books

Preview:

Every town has one. A big old house that has stood empty for so long, no one remembers anyone living there. The iconic subject of lore and folktales that hints at supernatural occurrences, tragedy, and family curses that can be neither confirmed nor denied. For the town of White Eagle, Montana, the house that serves as the subject of ghostly stories by the campfire is a huge old mansion built more than sixty years ago by a wealthy industrialist as a country home for his wife and five children. The house, devoid of love and laughter, served as a sort of luxury prison far away from the hustle and bustle of Hartford Harrington's full and busy life in San Francisco.

Structurally, Harrington House had weathered the long winters and hot summers of northern Montana. It had endured long after all but one of those five children had been buried in the little family cemetery at the edge of the huge estate. I'm not sure why the place was never sold, or even lived in, by whichever Harrington relation inherited the property, but after the summer Houston Harrington jumped from the third-floor window to the concrete bricks of the veranda below, not a single Harrington or heir had set foot in the place.

"Morning, Tess, Tilly," greeted Hap Hollister, as my golden retriever and I entered his home and hardware store to deliver the daily mail, along with a generous dollop of local news.

"I love the Halloween decorations you put in the window. The cobwebs and spiders are very believable," I jumped right in after setting the stack of mail I'd brought on the counter.

"I hope not too believable." Hap chuckled. "I wouldn't want to scare away potential customers."

"Combined with the big orange pumpkins and jolly scarecrow, I think the window is just right. It's very inviting."

Hap picked up the mail I had set on the counter and began thumbing through it. "Glad to hear it. I noticed your mom did her window up right nice too."

"As you're aware, the Halloween town Mom and Aunt Ruthie displays is a White Eagle tradition. It does seem the train Aunt Ruthie sent away for added a nice element this year."

"And that new haunted mansion she set off to the side. I love that the lights inside flash and there's a crackling sound every now and then that provides a very spooky feel."

"I guess every Halloween town needs a spooky Halloween house." I leaned a hip against the counter as Tilly sat patiently at my feet. "Speaking of spooky Halloween houses, did you hear someone moved into the Harrington place?"

"You don't say. About time someone brought some life to it. She's much too grand a lady to sit empty and unloved for so long."

I rested my elbows on the counter and leaned in. "Maybe, but everyone says it's haunted. I'm not sure why anyone would buy a haunted old house in the middle of nowhere."

Hap's blue eyes, faded with age, sparkled as he leaned his head of white hair in closer to my brown mane. "Guess there are some folks who either don't believe in ghosts, or aren't scared of them if they do. Personally, I like to think I rank among the latter."

My head tilted with curiosity. "So you believe in ghosts?"

Hap nodded. "Have to. Seen a few. Do you know anything about the new owner?"

"His name is Jordan Westlake. He's thirty-two, single, and, from what I hear, quite the babe."

"Babe?"

"He's handsome. In a cute and charming sort of way. I hear he's loaded and has plans to completely renovate the house from top to bottom."

Hap's eyes grew two sizes. "You don't say. Seems as the only home and hardware store in town, I might want to introduce myself to him. I'm sure Mr.

Westlake is going to be needing supplies. Paint and such."

I grinned. "I'm sure he will. Bree told me that Westlake is related to the San Francisco Westlakes and one of the heirs to Walter Westlake's fortune." Bree Price was a bookstore owner and my best friend and had taken the time to look him up. "I figured if he's that rich he'll just hire a contractor, but Bree said she read a newspaper article that said he plans to do a lot of the work on the house himself, only hiring out the plumbing, electrical, and heavy hauling. From what Bree was able to sleuth out, it looks like Jordan Westlake is, and always has been, rich enough so he never needed to work, so he took up a hobby: restoring old things and giving them new life."

"I'm anxious to meet this young man. He sounds like the sort I'd get along with just fine. Coffee?" Hap nodded toward the pot on his counter.

"Thanks, but I really should run. I'm supposed to hang out with Tony tonight and I don't want to be late."

"If you're going to see Tony, tell him that paint he ordered for his own remodel is in. I was going to call him, but the boy never seems to answer his dang blasted phone."

I laughed. "You know how it is when there's a genius at work. The rest of the world sort of fades away. I'll let him know about the paint."

After I left Hap's, I headed across the street to the White Eagle Police Station. My brother, Mike Thomas, should be in his office at this time of day, which meant I could firm up plans for tomorrow while delivering his mail. Mike, Bree, Tony, and I all planned to have dinner together at a new restaurant that had just opened up down by the lake. I also wanted to speak to his partner, Frank Hudson. I wondered if he had any information regarding White Eagle's newest resident. Frank, you see, in addition to be an all-around nice guy, excellent cop, and Mike's best friend, was a bit of a gossip. I was pretty sure if there was news, he'd be the one to ask about it.

"Morning, Frank," I greeted as I dropped his mail on his desk.

"Morning, Tess, Tilly."

"Any news on the newest member of our community?"

Frank leaned forward and lowered his voice, although we were the only two in the room. "I heard Jordan Westlake arrived in town yesterday afternoon, and according to Toby Tanner, who we know is a bit of a snoop, he spent the whole night holed up inside that huge, dusty old house."

"Really?" I had to admit I was surprised. I guess I just imagined a rich man would stay in a hotel while the place was being renovated. "Was the electricity and water even on?"

"Water and gas were turned on yesterday. Electricity will be on today. Toby said Westlake showed up with a fancy SUV filled with all sorts of camping equipment. It looks as if he plans to set up a tent in the middle of his living room."

I couldn't help but frown. "How exactly does Toby know all this?"

"Toby's been camping in the woods just behind the house. He brought his binoculars and enough food to last a week. He said he wanted to be in a position to see everything that went on from the very beginning."

"Does Mr. Westlake know he has a man with binoculars squatting on his property?"

Frank shrugged. "He hasn't lodged a complaint. If he does, I guess I'll have to run Toby off. In the meantime, I admit to being curious to find out what, if anything, he's able to see. He even brought a video recorder, which he promised to use only if a ghost shows up."

"Does Mike know about all this?" My brother was a bit more of a stickler for the rules than Frank, and I could see how he might object to Toby basically stalking Westlake.

"Haven't talked to him about it, but I haven't kept it from him either. Guess he might have heard something along the way. What he knows and what he doesn't know isn't a concern of mine."

I lifted a brow. "I sort of think Mike's going to see things differently. You should tell him what you know before he finds out from someone else."

"Someone else like you?" Frank said with a tone of accusation in his voice.

I held up my hands in my own defense. "I'm not saying a word. I am saying, though, that someone other than me might decide to tell Mike what's going on out at the old mansion."

Frank made a face. "I suppose I might mention it to him if it comes up in conversation."

I picked up my mailbag and prepared to head down the hallway to Mike's office. "Did Toby happen to mention what he observed last night?"

"Lights. Like from a candle or a flashlight, wandering from one room to the next for hours."

I shifted my bag onto my shoulder. "I guess Jordan Westlake might have been taking a look at his new place. Seems crazy to do it in the dark, though."

Frank winked. "Didn't say it was him causing the light to move around the house."

"You think someone else is there?"

"Some*one* or some*thing*."

I wasn't sure if I believed in ghosts, but I was pretty sure that if there were one or more living in the Harrington mansion, they wouldn't need a flashlight to see to get around. I was willing to bet Frank knew that as well. If I had to guess, he was just trying to scare me, but Tess Thomas didn't scare easily.

"Morning, Mike," I said after tapping three times on his open door.

He looked up from the report he was reading. "Morning, Tess, Tilly."

I set Mike's mail on his desk, then sat down on the chair across the desk from him. "Heard Jordan Westlake arrived yesterday."

"Yeah, I heard too."

"I'm kind of interested to meet him. From what Bree said, he's handsome and rich, but he must also be unique to have bought such a rundown old house with plans to renovate it with his own hands."

"Bree said he was handsome and rich?"

I lifted a shoulder. "Everyone is saying it."

Mike sighed.

"Can you blame them?" I added. "Having someone buy that old place and actually move in to it after all these years is the most interesting thing to happen in White Eagle for quite some time."

"He didn't buy it," Mike said.

I tilted my head. "He didn't buy it?"

"He inherited it. His mother was a Harrington before she married a Westlake. She was the closest heir, and she left the house to her youngest son, Jordan."

"I thought none of the five Harrington offspring married or had children. That's the story I've heard my whole life anyway. It seemed every one of those five children died before reaching adulthood. Houston Harrington, the youngest and last survivor, was just fourteen when he jumped from the third-floor window and killed himself."

"As far as I know that's true, but it seems Francine Westlake was adopted by Hartford Harrington when he married his second wife, Anastasia Pembroke, who had a daughter from a previous relationship."

"Wait." I held up a hand. "What happened to Hartford's first wife? The mother of the five children?"

"She died, most say of a broken heart, shortly after moving into the house."

Wow. This really was a depressing story. I wasn't sure I wanted to hear the rest, but I did want to hear about Jordan Westlake. "Okay, so Francine Harrington became Hartford Harrington's heir and married a Westlake."

"Donovan Westlake. Donovan Westlake and Francine Harrington have four sons. Jordan is the youngest. Francine Harrington Westlake recently passed, and in her will she left Harrington House to Jordan. I guess he isn't overly bothered by the fact that six people all related to him by adoption died while living in that house more than fifty years ago."

"Given the fact that he's here now, I guess not."

I stood up and slipped my bag back onto my shoulder. As interesting as this conversation was, I needed to get a move on if I was going to finish my route in time to go home and change before heading out to Tony's. "Are we still planning to meet at Bree's tomorrow night?"

"Short of an emergency, I'll be there."

I motioned to Tilly, then headed back down the hallway. Mike and Bree had settled into a committed relationship over the past few months. At first, I'll admit it felt odd that my brother and my best friend had feelings for each other, but after watching them together and realizing I'd never seen either of them happier, I found myself pulling for them to make it as a couple. Of course, it also made me nervous, and my nervousness made me spend quite a lot of time wondering if it was wise for friends to become intimate. Tony had told me that, in his opinion, friendship could be the basis for the most powerful love two people can have. His words rang true, but I worried that if Mike and Bree's relationship didn't stand the test of time, the comfortable companionship we'd all had since childhood would never be the same.

I thought back to my own almost pivotal moment with Tony, who, other than Bree, was my very best friend. I wasn't sure where the moment had come from, but on the same day Mike and Bree got together last spring, Tony and I found ourselves on the verge of bringing our own sexual tension to its logical conclusion. I've thought about it at least a million times since, and wondered what would have happened if Tony's dog, Titan, hadn't lumbered over and ruined the moment. Part of me was disappointed the kiss hadn't happened, but mostly, I was glad we hadn't taken a step that might lead to the end of the friendship we'd always had.

Bree thought I was crazy for not following through with my intensifying feelings for Tony, but I'd seen friendships ruined after sex was introduced into the relationship. Inevitably, the passion of new intimacy faded, and then all that remained of what was once a strong bond were hurt feelings that could never be overcome. No, I'd decided on numerous occasions, my feelings for Tony were too important to gamble on.

"Morning, Mom, Aunt Ruthie," I said as I walked into their diner, with Tilly tagging along behind me. It really did look festive. In addition to the Halloween village and model train in the window, Mom had strung up orange lights that were wrapped in colorful fall garlands.

"Is there mail from overseas?" Mom started hopefully.

I shook my head. "Sorry." My mom had been hoping for a card or letter from her own complicated love interest, Romero Montenegro. He lived and worked in Italy, but he and Mom had participated in a brief long-distance relationship that, based on the lack of correspondence in more than two months, seemed to have fizzled out.

"I should have taken the time off and gone to Italy when he asked." Mom groaned.

I wanted to remind her that her fling with Romero had been ill-advised from the beginning, but instead I held my tongue and gave her a hug. "I'm sorry, Mom. I know you enjoyed your friendship with him."

Mom let out a breath. "I suppose it's for the best. It's not like we ever had a future. I live here in Montana and he lives across the ocean." Mom gave a sad little smile. "It was fun while it lasted."

I didn't want her to be sad, but I also didn't want to think about my middle-aged mother having *fun* with a single playboy more than a decade younger, so I changed the subject. "Did you hear Jordan Westlake is in town?"

"I heard he arrived yesterday," Aunt Ruthie trilled. "People have been talking about it all day."

"I still don't quite understand what he plans to do with that huge old house," Mom said. "It doesn't seem like a practical choice for a single man."

"According to Mike, he didn't choose it. It chose him."

Mom frowned, confused.

"He inherited it," I clarified.

"Inherited it? I wonder if he means to keep it."

I shrugged. "The thing interests me more than I feel it ought to. Everyone says the place is haunted, and I've heard the story about the tragedy that met the family for whom the house was built. I'm not sure I'd set foot in it if that had happened to mine."

"I seem to remember Hartford Harrington moved his wife and children into the place but then went back to his life in the city," Aunt Ruthie said.

Mom nodded. "It's true. And they stayed even after the daughter went missing just two months after they arrived."

"Missing?" I asked. "I'd heard all the children died. I didn't know one went missing. What happened?"

"The oldest daughter, Hillary Harrington, was just fourteen when they moved into the big house in the woods. I'm not sure why they moved to White Eagle from San Francisco in the first place, but I do remember reading that after Hartford Harrington went back to the city, strange things began happening. The locals believed the family had brought some sort of curse with them from San Francisco. I don't know if that's true, but two months after they came to town, Hillary Harrington went missing. Her bloody clothes were found in the woods behind the house. It was assumed she'd met with foul play, but her body was never found and her killer, if there was one, was never identified."

I put a hand to my mouth. "That's awful. The poor girl. Her poor mother."

Mom ran a rag over the counter of the currently empty café. "I can't imagine losing a child and never knowing what happened to her. It has to be more heartbreaking than is bearable. But she not only lost a daughter but her oldest son just a few weeks later."

I gasped. "How?"

"He was shot."

My eyes grew large. "Who shot him?"

"A man named Wilbur Woodbine. It seems Hudson Harrington believed it was Wilbur who'd killed his sister and hid her body, so even though he was only sixteen and Wilbur was a grown man, he went to confront him. Hudson had a gun, but so did Wilbur. In the end, it was Hudson who lost his life."

"And Wilbur?" I asked. "What happened to him?"

Mom shook her head. "Nothing. There was never any proof he'd killed Hillary, and it was decided the shooting was in self-defense."

I glanced at the clock. I wanted to hear the rest of the story, but I had my route to finish. "How do you know all this?" I asked as I hitched my bag onto my shoulder.

"I did a report on the family when I was in high school. I can fill you in on the rest sometime, but I can see you need to get back to work, so I won't keep you."

I took a step toward the door. "I'll come by tomorrow."

Books by Kathi Daley

Come for the murder, stay for the romance.

Zoe Donovan Cozy Mystery:
Halloween Hijinks
The Trouble With Turkeys
Christmas Crazy
Cupid's Curse
Big Bunny Bump-off
Beach Blanket Barbie
Maui Madness
Derby Divas
Haunted Hamlet
Turkeys, Tuxes, and Tabbies
Christmas Cozy
Alaskan Alliance
Matrimony Meltdown
Soul Surrender
Heavenly Honeymoon
Hopscotch Homicide
Ghostly Graveyard
Santa Sleuth
Shamrock Shenanigans
Kitten Kaboodle
Costume Catastrophe
Candy Cane Caper
Holiday Hangover
Easter Escapade
Camp Carter
Trick or Treason
Reindeer Roundup

Hippity Hoppity Homicide
Firework Fiasco
Henderson House – *August 2018*

Zimmerman Academy The New Normal
Ashton Falls Cozy Cookbook

Tj Jensen Paradise Lake Mysteries:
Pumpkins in Paradise
Snowmen in Paradise
Bikinis in Paradise
Christmas in Paradise
Puppies in Paradise
Halloween in Paradise
Treasure in Paradise
Fireworks in Paradise
Beaches in Paradise

Whales and Tails Cozy Mystery:
Romeow and Juliet
The Mad Catter
Grimm's Furry Tail
Much Ado About Felines
Legend of Tabby Hollow
Cat of Christmas Past
A Tale of Two Tabbies
The Great Catsby
Count Catula
The Cat of Christmas Present
A Winter's Tail
The Taming of the Tabby
Frankencat
The Cat of Christmas Future
Farewell to Felines

A Whisker in Time – *September 2018*

Writers' Retreat Seashore Mystery:
First Case
Second Look
Third Strike
Fourth Victim
Fifth Night
Sixth Cabin
Seventh Chapter – *August 2018*

Rescue Alaska Paranormal Mystery:
Finding Justice
Finding Answers
Finding Courage – *September 2018*

A Tess and Tilly Mystery:
The Christmas Letter
The Valentine Mystery
The Mother's Day Mishap
The Halloween House – *July 2018*

Haunting by the Sea:
Homecoming by the Sea
Secrets by the Sea

Sand and Sea Hawaiian Mystery:
Murder at Dolphin Bay
Murder at Sunrise Beach
Murder at the Witching Hour
Murder at Christmas
Murder at Turtle Cove
Murder at Water's Edge

Murder at Midnight

Seacliff High Mystery:
The Secret
The Curse
The Relic
The Conspiracy
The Grudge
The Shadow
The Haunting

Road to Christmas Romance:
Road to Christmas Past

USA Today best-selling author Kathi Daley lives in beautiful Lake Tahoe with her husband Ken. When she isn't writing, she likes spending time hiking the miles of desolate trails surrounding her home. She has authored more than seventy-five books in nine series, including Zoe Donovan Cozy Mysteries, Whales and Tails Island Mysteries, Sand and Sea Hawaiian Mysteries, Tj Jensen Paradise Lake Series, Writers' Retreat Southern Seashore Mysteries, Rescue Alaska Paranormal Mysteries, Haunting By The Sea Paranormal Mysteries, and Seacliff High Teen Mysteries. Find out more about her books at **www.kathidaley.com**

Stay up to date:

Newsletter, *The Daley Weekly*
http://eepurl.com/NRPDf
Webpage – **www.kathidaley.com**
Facebook at Kathi Daley Books –
www.facebook.com/kathidaleybooks
Kathi Daley Books Group Page –
https://www.facebook.com/groups/5695788231468 50/
E-mail – **kathidaley@kathidaley.com**
Twitter at Kathi Daley@kathidaley –
https://twitter.com/kathidaley
Amazon Author Page –
https://www.amazon.com/author/kathidaley
BookBub –
https://www.bookbub.com/authors/kathi-daley

42003903R00102

Made in the USA
Middletown, DE
10 April 2019